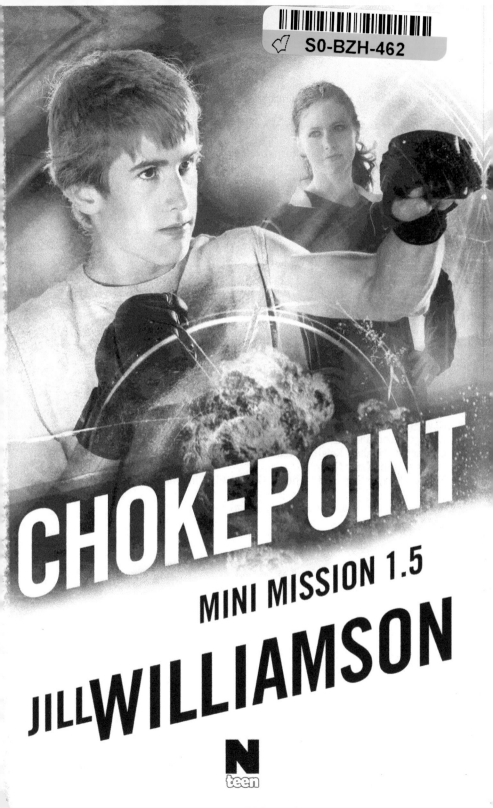

CHOKEPOINT

MINI MISSION 1.5

JILL WILLIAMSON

N
teen

The author is represented by MacGregor Literary Inc. of Hillsboro, OR.

Cover Designer: Kirk DouPonce
Editor: Rebecca Luella Miller
Character Sketches: Keighley Kendig
ebook design: Kerry Nietz
Mission League Logo and Fighting Sketch: Jill Williamson

International Standard Book Number: 978-0-9887594-0-4

Printed in the United States of America

To the Haydon family.

Spencer

Gabe

Arianna

Nick

Isaac

Isabel

Jensina

Jake

Beth

RESTRICTED ACCESS

YOU HAVE ACCESSED THE
INTERNATIONAL SERVER FOR
THE MISSION LEAGUE.

THESE FILES CONTAIN CLASSIFIED INFORMATION
ON THE ORGANIZATION, AGENTS, CRIMINALS, PROCEDURES,
TRAININGS AND MISSIONS.

GOD HAS CALLED. YOU HAVE ANSWERED.

REPORT NUMBER: 1

REPORT TITLE: I Get Beat by a Girl
SUBMITTED BY: Agent-in-Training Spencer Garmond
LOCATION: Intersection of Fifth and Rose, Pilot Point,
California, USA
DATE AND TIME: Monday, October 13, 2:51 p.m.

THE VISIONS WERE HAPPENING MORE frequently, but that didn't mean I was used to them—especially when they popped up in the middle of the day.

The headache came first, then the vision. The scene surged into my mind, leaving me winded and tense, the way standing too close to the freeway did when a big rig drove by.

I kicked a pebble into the bushes and continued down the sidewalk of Fifth Street on my way home from school, my basketball tucked under one arm. Now I was faced with a choice. Confront what I'd seen or run.

I used to think my visions showed me inevitable events, that they predicted my future or someone else's. But in Moscow, I'd learned that they were possibilities. So today, because of my vision, I knew that cutting through the park would bring me face to face with C-Rok and his gang. They'd pick a fight by trying to steal my basketball. I'd fight back. It wouldn't end well.

Been there, done that.

But I had a choice. I could take the long way home and never run into C-Rok.

I stopped at the corner of Fifth and Rose and waited to cross—to head home around Alameda Park—the long and safe way. I spun my basketball on my finger. Life was getting pretty boring without any surprises.

In the yard to my left, a bald man dressed as a gardener trimmed a hedge with a large pair of shears. He cut the same spot again and again, peering at me a little too often. Creeper.

The signal changed, and I crossed Fifth, scanning my surroundings with each step.

On the edge of the park, a tall, broad-shouldered man tramped a groove in the grass, dragging a feisty terrier on a leash. The guy had olive skin and a full head of black hair with a little extra poking out of his ears and nose. A sasquatch if I ever saw one. The terrier barked and nipped at the man's pant legs every so often.

So much for covert ops. Even the dog knew the guy wasn't normal. But maybe that's how the Mission League wanted it. Maybe they wanted the baddies to see that I had a flock of bodyguards around me at all times.

I glanced over my shoulder. A black town car with tinted windows crawled behind me. Kimbal and his chauffer with the crooked nose. I faced forward and kicked another rock.

Ever since I returned from Moscow, life was a full court press. Mission League Field agents were everywhere. All the time. Watching. Even the cross necklace that hung around my neck like a leash had a tracking device in the charm.

If I were famous or rich, I might feel differently about being guarded twenty-four/seven, but I knew of no legitimate reason for the agents to keep this up. So some crazy Russian criminal named Anya had said some creepy stuff. Big deal. She hadn't contacted me since Moscow.

What bothered me more than the fact that I might be in danger was that Anya probably knew more about me than I did—cue the creepy music.

At least now I knew "Spencer Garmond" was an alias the Mission League had given me years ago when they hid me in this California town. All I'd pieced together about my real identity was my first name, Jonas, and that my father was responsible for my mom's death. Everything I'd thought I knew about life before this summer had been a lie. And Grandma, Kimbal, Mr. S, Prière—no one would tell me squat.

Real nice, huh?

Kimbal's sedan sped past and turned on Maple, headed to Oak Street where I lived with my grandma, "Alice Garmond"— only that was likely an alias, too, since Anya had referred to her as Lorraine.

Again, the criminal knowing more about me than I did. What was up with that?

I dropped my ball to the sidewalk and started dribbling. The tiny bumps on the leather spun against my hand. With each bounce of the ball I forced the agents out of my thoughts and focused on my first League Combat Training lesson with Beth a few hours from now.

LCT was the Mission League's special form of combined martial arts. A smile came to my lips. I secretly relished this unexpected reward for my breaking protocol in Moscow and my loss of personal League points. Taking LCT lessons was going to be ah-some.

The sedan was parked on the street in front of Grandma's house when I dribbled up the driveway. Dave Kimbal sat on the porch swing, wearing a pair of jeans and the Lakers T-shirt I'd given him for his birthday last month. I stopped, brought the ball up, and shot it straight into his lap.

He caught the ball and chuckled. "What's got you so peppy?"

I climbed the steps and sat next to my uncle—my dad's brother. I was still getting used to *that* realization, but Kimbal's pale freckled skin and carrot-orange hair made it easier to believe. The dude used to be my school resource officer, but I didn't need an SRO. Anymore.

I pushed back, and the porch swing shook. "I start LCT today."

Kimbal frowned. "I thought you can't take LCT until you get your points up?"

"Technically, I'm not taking it." I snatched my ball back from Kimbal and spun it on my knee.

"Technically?" Kimbal raised his bushy orange eyebrow.

"Beth volunteered to train me. Mondays and Wednesdays."

"Watkins?" Kimbal laughed out loud. "*That*, I'd like to see. Should I send some guys along in case you get in trouble? She's one tough girl."

This I knew, but the mockery was unnecessary. "Why are you here?"

"Just a protocol visit. Wondering if you've seen anything odd lately?"

I scrolled though the many ways I could answer that question. "Nothing odder than usual. Nothing odder than four agents following me everywhere. The *gardener* chased me into the bathroom today after lunch. That's just wrong."

"Gardener?"

"I've given them all names. The bald guy with the hedge clippers is Gardener. The hairy guy with the dog is Sasquatch. And your driver is Nose."

"How very original. No weird, creepy feelings like you had in Moscow?"

"Nope." Weird, creepy feelings were different from my visions. Weird, creepy feelings meant trouble. Demon trouble, according to my churcher friend Arianna Sloan.

"Well, good." Kimbal stood. "I gotta run. We still on for ball this Saturday?"

"I wouldn't miss a chance to cream you."

"For your sake, I hope you do cream me. You'll need some pride redemption after LCT today. I've seen what Watkins can do to guys like you."

Guys like me? "What's that supposed to mean?"

"You'll see." Kimbal jogged down the porch steps and looked back. "Sure you don't need a lift?"

"I'll walk, thanks."

"What about a ride home? You could be in bad shape after."

Like getting a ride with Kimbal mattered. He would follow me anyway, like he had every day for the past thirteen years. "Get lost, will you?"

Kimbal chuckled and walked toward the black sedan. I went inside the house, tossed my ball on Grandma's velour armchair, and bee-lined to the kitchen. I slathered peanut butter onto slices of wheat bread until I'd made three hefty sandwiches. I licked the knife, tossed it in the sink, and took my snack to my room. My eyes shifted straight for the digital clock half hanging off the shelf next to my bed. Only two hours until I was supposed to meet Beth.

I had no idea what to wear for my first beating.

• • •

"Attack me."

I blinked. "Serious?"

Beth, her brown hair secured in a ponytail, stood across the mat from me, barefoot, dressed in a pair of black combat pants and a white T-shirt that said, "Caution: Next mood swing in five minutes." She held out her hands, palms up, and beckoned me. "Yes. Try and take me down, Tiger."

My stomach flipped every time she called me "Tiger." I took one step forward and stopped. I didn't want to hurt her.

"It's called grappling. Or sparring. It's how we practice." She pointed at me. "You're the bad guy, and you want to attack me. So do it. Now."

I scanned the room. The LCT training facility, also known as C Camp, was located at 95 Juniper in a non-descript brick office building with no sign out front. The guard had only let me in because Beth had put my name on "the list." Once I'd passed through the men's locker room, I'd discovered that the place was like an athletic club with mats and punching bags instead of stair climbers and exercise bikes. A couple weight benches sat off to one side.

At least Beth and I were alone. I mean, nice that she thought I was concerned I might hurt her. But she was a tough chick, and I didn't want to get whipped in front of an audience.

Maybe I could play on that concern. "Okay . . ." I inched toward her, wearing what I hoped was my most pathetic and worrisome expression. "But what if . . .?" Two more steps. "I'm just not really sure how to, you know . . ." Another step. I was two yards away now.

She put her hands on her hips and blew a loose wisp of hair out of her eyes. "Stop whining. What kind of opponent are you gonna be if you—"

I rushed forward, blitzing like a linebacker. I wrapped both arms around Beth's waist and threw all my weight against her. We fell. Adrenaline surged inside. I was winning. See? I could handle myself against—

Uh oh.

Beth rolled into a backwards somersault, pulling me with her. I caught a glimpse of my bare feet in the air. My head filled with pressure.

I hit the mat like an egg in a science experiment. *Oof.*

Beth was sitting on top of me—sweet! But her forearm crushed my neck in a vise that bordered on choking. I kicked my legs, but they only flailed about, hitting nothing.

How pathetic.

Beth's eyes stared into mine, fierce green and catlike; her lips twisted in a smirk. "Distraction. Nice try, Tiger, but you gave up control of your weight, and I used it against you." She held her position. "Tap out."

I turned my wrist until I could slap the mat with my palm. Beth released me and popped to her feet. I scrambled to mine before she tried anything.

"Where'd you get the Special Forces duds, anyway?" she asked me.

I looked down at my tan T-shirt and fatigues. "They gave them to me in Moscow."

"*They* who?"

"Jake and the Scene Investigation Department people."

Beth crouched down beside me and rubbed the hem of my pants between her fingers. "Lucky dog. These are real BDUs."

"BDU?"

"Battle dress utility." Beth stood and placed her feet apart on the mat. She bent her knees. "Let's go again."

I circled her slowly, heart thudding in my chest. I had no clue what I was doing. Wasn't she going to teach me anything? That was why I was here—I wanted to learn.

Beth closed her eyes. "Come *on*, Spencer. I won't even look."

"What's the point? So you're better than me. Teach me something so I can actually fight you." I didn't mind her pinning me—it was fun. But I didn't want to look like a wimp, either.

At Beth's slight smile, a dimple formed in one cheek. Her eyes were still closed. "I have my reasons."

I leapt forward and threw a punch, wincing the whole time. I so didn't want to hurt her.

Beth's eyes flicked open. She blocked my punch with her palm, grabbed my wrist, turned into me, and bent over. I twisted, rolled off her back, and landed flat on mine. My jarred brain ran an injury inventory. Loss of air to the lungs: major problem. Everything else: intact.

"Again. Get up." Beth clapped her hands in front of my face.

I flinched.

Thirty minutes later I felt the scowl burn into my face as Beth slung my body onto the mat for—I'd lost count of how many times. A million, maybe. I gritted my teeth as she walked away.

What was I doing wrong?

I scrambled to my feet and charged. I jumped on her, piggyback, and locked one arm around her neck. She sagged, but managed to hold my weight. She wedged her chin into the crook of my elbow and walked backwards. Her hands flew to my forearm, fingernails digging in, but I held on. I clenched my jaw, tensing against the sharp pain of nails cutting into flesh.

She flung herself back against the cement wall. My head bounced off the concrete with a dull thud. I winced and loosened my grip. It was enough for Beth to throw me again, sending my body rolling several times across the padded floor. I stopped on my stomach, face buried into the mat, eyes closed to merciful darkness, rubbing my scratched arm. I focused on the blackness of the inside of my eyelids.

"Okay, enough torture." Beth's voice seemed far away. "I can see I have my work cut out for me."

Brutal, emasculating female. I rolled over and found Beth standing over me, hands on her hips. I rose onto my elbows. "What's that supposed to mean?"

She flopped down beside me and sat cross-legged. "If you're going to learn LCT, you've got to separate your emotions from your actions—in your brain. If I throw a punch at you, your brain freaks out and thinks, 'A punch will hurt me.' Then your brain reverts to survival instincts and you do something dumb like you just did."

"That's the *best* I did."

"No. You lost control 'cause you were angry. People who fight from emotions don't fight smart. LCT isn't about hurting anyone. It's about accomplishing one of two objectives: subduing someone without harm or protecting yourself so you can get away."

I held up my arm so she could see her cat scratches. "How's this not harm?"

"I protected myself to get away. You were out of control and stronger than me. I did what I had to do to avoid getting choked."

"I'm *not* stronger than you."

Beth raised her eyebrows. "Yeah, you are. I just know how to use my muscles. Besides, it isn't always the size of the muscles; it's the size of the brain. If you fight smart, you'll fight best." She massaged her throat. "First you've got to separate your emotions from the experience. You can't think, 'I'm fighting Beth. I'm going to hurt her, or she's going to hurt me.' You've got to think about your objective. Subduing without harm or getting away."

"But how can you stay calm when someone's punching you?"

"I concentrate on the strike points."

I shook my head. The girl spoke nonsense.

Beth smiled big, both dimples emerging. "Don't worry. I'll teach you." She snagged a flyer off the wall and grabbed a pen from her bag. She flopped down on her stomach, flipped the flyer over, and began to draw. "Strike points work like this." Beth drew a stick man with numbers around him.

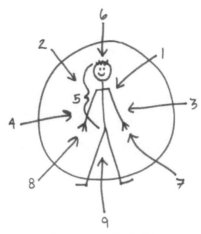

"Okay. Number one and two are high hits coming from the left or right. Number three and four hits come from the sides. Five is anything in the middle from a high five to the face to a low five to the groin. Six is straight down on the head, seven and eight are low hits from the ground, and a nine is between the legs."

I cringed.

Beth tapped the paper with the back of her pen. "Most attacks are a one, two, three, four, or five. You want to think about a hit in terms of the number it's coming from and not what it can do to you. This is what keeps you from panicking in a fight. Get it?"

"I think so." But why was her stick man smiling?

"Good." She slapped the paper against my chest. "Memorize that."

REPORT NUMBER: 2

REPORT TITLE: A Male Manicurist Saves My Neck
SUBMITTED BY: Agent-in-Training Spencer Garmond
LOCATION: 95 Juniper Avenue, Pilot Point, California
DATE AND TIME: Monday, October 13, 6:37 p.m.

I HOBBLED OUT OF C CAMP TOWARD THE intersection of juniper and First, carrying my backpack by the straps. It was almost dark. The black sedan at the curb started its engine and flipped on its headlights. I paused to glare at the tinted windows, knowing Kimbal and Nose were inside, watching.

If Beth hadn't forgotten to teach me breakfalls, I wouldn't have twisted my ankle. Thanks a lot, girl. Apparently, I was her first pupil ever.

The sedan's passenger window rolled down. "Need a lift?" Kimbal's voice oozed amusement.

I walked stiffly toward the corner, fighting the urge to limp. I wasn't about to give Kimbal the satisfaction of seeing me injured.

Why did the man have to follow me *every second*? Over two months had passed since Moscow and not a thing had happened to hint at trouble. It was getting ridiculous.

I ran a quick inventory of the surrounding area but only spotted one agent on foot. The Sasquatch and his scrawny dog lingered across the street. There were usually four—two in the car and two on foot.

Where was Gardener?

The sedan nosed its way to the intersection and the red light. I turned in a full circle looking for Gardener. Had they cut back to three agents?

A man in a black trench coat was standing at the signal on the corner. I stopped beside him and reached for the button to cross Juniper, but he beat me to it. Could this guy have replaced Gardener? I studied him. He was slim and tall and pale—like a vampire. A half dozen earrings edged one of his ears.

This was no agent. Piercings were against protocol. Plus this guy, at almost six feet tall, couldn't weigh more than one fifty. He was a blade of grass, not promising for a field agent. It could be a disguise, but I doubted much muscle hid under that coat.

The man gazed forward, ignoring my rude stare. I should look away, but I just couldn't. Something about this guy nagged at my brain, though I didn't think I'd ever seen him before.

"Want to lose them, Jonas?" the man asked in a smooth voice, continuing to stare forward.

I stepped back, surprised. "You're an agent?"

The blade of grass nodded toward Kimbal's car. "It'll give them something to do. My partner is just there." He nodded toward a black Range Rover in the turn lane on First. The left blinker flashed yellow light across the dark pavement. "We'll go for Starbucks. That's what you kids are into these days, right? Fancy coffee?"

My spine tingled. This guy wanted me to get into his car? I wondered if there was some sort of standard passcode to identify agents in Pilot Point. Why hadn't Kimbal given me one? "I don't drink coffee."

"So we'll get a milkshake or a soda—whatever you want."

Across the street the red hand changed to a white figure. The man glanced at me as he stepped off the curb. His eyes were dark. "Let's go."

The man crossed, but I stayed put, watching Kimbal's car drive away. The blade of grass reached the other side and kept going. The little white man switched to a flashing red hand. I walked across, taking my time. The light changed just as I stepped up on the sidewalk. The Range Rover turned the corner—its headlights blinding me for a moment—and pulled up along the curb a few yards ahead where the blade of grass was waiting.

The guy opened the passenger door and looked my way. "Coming?"

Not on your life, buddy. But Kimbal's car was already down the block, stopped at the next intersection. I glanced at Sasquatch and found him looking at me, the little dog tucked under his arm like a football. His lips moved. He was either talking to himself, praying, or talking to someone on a radio. I hoped it was Kimbal.

Sasquatch shook his head at me. No. Don't get in the car.

Good plan.

I took his advice and sprinted up First. Tires squealed on the street behind me. The Range Rover? I didn't look back. My ankle sent protesting stabs of pain up my leg with every stride. I tightened my hold on my backpack and booked it to the next intersection.

Across the street, the hair salon, *Peluqueria Rodriguez*, owned by Isabel's mom, caught my eye. A streetlight splashed an amber ray onto the *open* sign in the door. I could duck in there and get someone to hide me. If not Isabel, then her mom. I'd only seen her once before, when she dropped Isabel at the airport before we left for Moscow. If Isabel wasn't there, hopefully her mom would remember me.

I pushed through the door. A bell attached to the top jingled. It was bright inside and smelled like girls. There were all kinds of hair-cutting stations and shelves packed with shampoo bottles, but no people.

"We close in ten minutes," a guy said.

I turned around. Almost no people. Two were sitting across from each other at a tiny table in the corner—a woman getting her nails done and a guy painting them.

Yeah, that's what I said. A guy. The dude looked about my age. He was wearing a black hoodie and a backwards red and black cap with the OBEY star above the snapback. He dipped the little paintbrush into some red polish and swiped it down one of the woman's fingernails. Then he glanced at me, and his eyebrows shot up his forehead. "Can I help you?"

"Uh . . ." I glanced out the windows, but the outside darkness had turned them into mirrors. All I could see was the reflection of myself standing in the salon. "Isabel?"

"Not here. And if you're looking to ask her out, she has a boyfriend."

This guy was Isabel's boyfriend? "Thanks, but no. How about her mom?"

"Also not here. I'm closing up today."

Great. I reached for the door, but it swung in. A Hispanic Incredible Hulk stepped inside. The man's face, neck, hands—everything—was covered in tattoos. I stared, mesmerized by the guy's inked skin. I mean, that was *a lot* of skin candy. He stared back as if daring me to make a comment. The gold chain around his neck could tow a car.

"*Cerramos en cinco minutos,*" the manicure kid said.

Tattoo Hulk grabbed my arm. "We were just leaving." His voice was low and muffled, like he wasn't getting enough oxygen for surround sound.

I tried to pull away, but the guy must have weighed three hundred pounds. He dragged me toward the door. I jabbed my elbow into his solar plexus, stomped on his foot . . . He didn't even flinch. Must have been made of metal.

"Call Isabel's mom," I told the kid. "Tell her Spencer Garmond is in trouble. No, call the cops."

The manicure kid stood up. "Excuse me, Mrs. Flores. I need to deal with this." He walked over to a shelf filled with bottles and grabbed one. He crossed to stand in front of the door. He couldn't have been more than five foot nine, David about to face Goliath before my very eyes. "Look, I don't want any trouble," the kid said to Tattoo Hulk. "Let him go, or I'm going to have to hurt you."

Tattoo Hulk swung at the kid, who ducked, then popped the cap on the bottle in his hand and sprayed the monster's eyes.

Tattoo Hulk released me and doubled over, pawing at his face. The kid opened the door, set his foot against the monster's backside, and pushed. Tattoo Hulk stumbled onto the sidewalk. The kid slammed the door and turned the lock. Then he flipped the sign in the window from *open* to *closed*.

Whoa.

"Take a seat," the kid said to me. "If he doesn't leave, I'll call the cops."

I sat on a chair in front of a table covered in hair magazines.

The kid picked up the cap from the floor, put it back on the bottle, and returned the bottle to the shelf. Then he sat back down at the table and picked up Mrs. Flores's hand. "Sorry about that, Mrs. Flores. I'm almost done."

"*¡Qué grosero!*" Mrs. Flores said. "For that man to come in here and try to attack your sister's friend . . ."

"Sister?" I said. This was Isabel's little brother?

"Oh, *sí*," Mrs. Flores told me. "Lukas *es muy valiente*."

Lukas dipped the nail brush back into the little bottle. "I've dealt with worse."

I raised my eyebrows. "Really? Because that guy was massive, and you didn't even flinch."

"He's got nothing on my Uncle Marcos. Or Mrs. Lopez's ex. Every time Mrs. Lopez comes in to get her roots done, her ex shows up."

Mrs. Flores gasped. "I thought *Abella* had . . . *¿como se dice?. . . un* restraint ruling against that *hombre*."

Lukas snorted. "She does. But he knows she gets her hair done here, so he's always watching this place."

Someone rapped on the door. Lukas got up and went to take a look. "Your SRO is here," he said, flipping the lock.

I stood up. "He's not my SRO." Besides, after starting the school year with my three-day suspension from last year's fight, I hadn't even gotten a detention so far this year.

Kimbal came in. "Spencer, what are you doing?"

"Just hanging out with Lukas and Mrs. Flores. Thought maybe I'd get a haircut."

"Get your stuff, chuckles. The car's out front." Kimbal left, slamming the door behind him. The bell jangled.

I stepped toward the door. "Hey, thanks for the . . . you know . . . hairspray."

"No problem," Lukas said. "And you remember what I said about my sister."

"Yeah, well, you don't have to worry about me." Anymore.

As I left the salon, I heard Lukas say, "Now if I could just get Isabel to dump her loser boyfriend."

The sedan was idling at the curb. I scanned the sidewalk but saw no sign of the Incredible Tattooed Hulk. I climbed into the back. Kimbal sat in the passenger's seat. He stared at me as I got in, and the look on his face could melt rubber.

Kimbal stared straight ahead. "You okay?"

I shut the door. "Yeah." But not really. Two random freaks had just tried to abduct me. I didn't like that word, *abduct*. It sounded like something that happened to helpless kids and girls. Plus my ankle hurt. I rotated it in a circle. Not so bad, I guess. A little ice, a compression wrap, and I'd be in good shape for basketball tryouts.

"My guy followed you," Kimbal said. "He was out front. But when the Land Rover drove up and the big guy came out of the salon alone, my guy decided not to engage. What happened in there? What'd he say?"

I told Kimbal about the blade of grass offering *Jonas* a ride, how I'd tried to hide out in Isabel's mom's shop, and how her brother had maced Tattoo Hulk with hairspray. "You think this has to do with Anya or my dad?"

"Don't know."

Sure he didn't. Those guys had looked like Anya's breed. But I didn't know anything about my dad. "What was he like? My dad?"

Kimbal didn't turn around, and I figured he wasn't going to answer. But he finally said, "Everybody liked your dad. He made people laugh."

Really. "I guess he just didn't want to be a father, then."

"No," Kimbal said. "I don't know what your grandma told you, but it probably wasn't true. She had to make something up for her cover story, you know."

"She said he left us. But she never said why. She hates my dad, though. And you said he betrayed my mom and got her killed, so I guess Grandma has a right."

"Look. Your dad messed up. But he never left your mom. He never left you."

Never left? "But before you said—"

"Just drop it, okay?"

No. Not okay. Whether or not my dad was a scumbag mattered to me. I stared out the window. "I deserve to know what happened. Why those guys tried to nab me." Nab was a much better word than *abduct* or *kidnap*.

Kimbal sighed. "It's not my call and you know it. Prière is in St. Louis right now. I can't promise anything, but I think he'll talk to you soon."

I slouched in the seat. *Soon* was the best answer I'd gotten out of Kimbal yet. International Headquarters for the Mission

League was located in St. Louis, Missouri. If Prière was there, maybe they'd finally give him permission to tell me something about my dad.

Something true.

• • •

My investigation into my parent's past hadn't gone far. Since I didn't know their real names, all I had to go on was the tip Nick had given me in Moscow: a building that had blown up in Los Angeles twelve or thirteen years ago. "Blew up" got me nowhere on Google. But "explosion" got some hits. Still, online newspapers only seemed to give breaking news, so for all of my leads, I couldn't find any follow-up stories.

That night I made a list of events which might fit, even if an intelligence organization had given the press a bogus story. That left me with four: "Woman killed after underground explosion in Westlake," "Two dead and three injured in South L.A. explosion," "Fatal explosion near downtown L.A. kills three," and "Gas cylinder explosion leaves one dead, injures five."

None of the stories gave the names of the dead or injured. LAPD Online said I could only order a crime report if I was an authorized person, like the victim or the victim's lawyer.

How about the dead victim's son?

They probably wouldn't give one to a minor anyway. Plus I didn't have any case numbers. I needed a plan B.

Kip. Having a best friend whose dad was a police officer in Pilot Point might come in handy. Maybe I could talk him into helping me.

It was worth a shot.

REPORT NUMBER: 3

REPORT TITLE: I Ask a Cop for Help
SUBMITTED BY: Agent-in-Training Spencer Garmond
LOCATION: Kip Johnson's House at 733 Elm Street, Pilot
Point, California
DATE AND TIME: Tuesday, October 14, 5:24 p.m.

KIP LIVED ON SNOB HILL IN A SPRAWLING, one-story
beige house with a Spanish tile roof. Kip and I sat in the living
room in the dark, taking turns playing Torch, a first-person
action game that he had just bought. He'd logged in online too,
which was stupid since he didn't know how to play yet. Every
two steps someone killed him.

"These guys are pretty bad," Kip said.

"*You're* bad." I walked into the kitchen and opened the
pantry cupboard.

"Seriously. They're not even playing," Kip said. "It's like
they're playing with blindfolds."

"What are you talking about? You're getting killed every two steps."

"Not even Sammy played this bad."

"Whatever." Sammy, our other best friend, lived in Sacramento with his mom ever since his dad had been indicted as a drug dealer. The plan was for him to move back home after the trial, assuming his dad would be acquitted.

I carried a bag of chips to the couch. Kip had just entered the mythical cavern. "Get the sword. Dude. Turn around. Kip, turn around."

Kip ignored me.

"No, I need to show you something." I said. "It's really important. Go outside."

"I have a gun. I don't need a sword."

"Yes, you do. It's special. Go get it."

Kip's iPhone buzzed. The screen glowed from where it sat beside him on the couch. He glanced at it, then back at the TV. "I don't care about the sword."

I pointed at the cavern exit. "It's over there. Go get it. Go— you died again!"

Kip dropped the controller and picked up his phone. On screen, his man just stood there, crouched. "How did I die? I don't even understand." Kip started texting.

"That was a spellcaster," I said. "He threw a death spell and . . . What are you doing?"

"Meagan's texting me."

I reached for the controller. "If you're not going to play, let me."

Kip dropped his phone and snatched up the controller. "I'm playing." His guy continued through the cavern.

Dumb fool needed to get the sword. I opened the chips and ate a few. Kip's phone buzzed again, but he shot at some troll.

"Yeah! Got him. Right there, baby! Were you watching? Did you see that?"

"Yeah, I saw. You killed a troll. Congratulations. That's not the first time someone has killed a troll in this game."

"Yeah, but . . ." He glanced at his phone. "It's one more troll than *you* killed."

"I've killed, like, a hundred trolls," I said.

"What? When did you kill a hundred trolls? I just got this game. I just opened the package today." Kip texted something, then went back to the game.

I ate another chip. "Texting and playing? No wonder you keep dying."

"When did you kill a hundred trolls, Spencer?"

"A demo at Game Masters."

Kip's phone buzzed again. He glanced at it but kept playing. "You played a Game Masters demo for two hours?"

"I lost track of time." I snatched Kip's phone. "What is she texting you that's so important?"

I read the screen. *kewl. gues what?*

"That's it? You keep dying for this conversation?"

"Text her back. Ask her: 'What?' "

"Fine. If it gets you through this level so I can play." I texted the one-word question.

"By the way," Kip said, "Meagan asked Trella if she'd go with you to homecoming."

"Trella Myers?" The girl was a cheerleader. Thought she was all that. She was kind of cute in a rich-girl, I'm-better-than-you sort of way.

But dancing . . . yeah. Not my favorite pastime. "I don't know . . ."

"It doesn't matter. Trella said you had ape arms and are too tall for her homecoming picture." Kip laughed.

Ouch. "*Ape* arms?" Who'd said I wanted to go to homecoming anyway?

Kip shrugged and shot at a troll.

I lifted Kip's cell phone and hit the contacts icon. "I'm going to text your stupid girlfriend and say: 'Thanks for nothing.'"

"Don't! It's not Meagan's fault that Trella's a troll." He fired at one on the screen. "Why won't they die?"

The front door opened. Kip's dad came in, dressed in his Pilot Point P.D. uniform. "Hey, guys."

"Die, ugly trolls!" Kip yelled.

"Hey, Mr. Johnson." I carried Kip's phone into the kitchen and sat on a stool at the counter. I couldn't help but stare at Mr. Johnson's belt. It was crammed with awesomeness: radio, gun, baton, cuffs, taser. "What kind of a gun is that?"

"Glock 40, semi-automatic."

Sweet. "Can I hold it?"

"No, you may not."

"Can I ask you something, Mr. Johnson?"

"*Doug*. Calling me *Mr. Johnson* makes me sound like an old man, and I've got a date tonight with a Victoria Secret model."

"Right, sorry." And, eww. But there was no way I could call a cop by his first name, at least not while he was wearing the blues. Kip's phone buzzed in my hand. I read the screen: *got nu shoes*.

"Seriously?" I turned on the barstool so I could see Kip. "Meagan got new shoes. What do I say to that?"

"I don't know. Make something up. But keep the conversation going. She gets mad if I don't answer."

Right. I spun back and texted, *What kind?*

"What was it you wanted to ask, Spencer?"

I looked up. Mr. Johnson was standing at the mouth of the hallway at the end of the kitchen, loosening his necktie. "Oh, sorry. Uh, I've been looking into my mom's death."

Mr. Johnson frowned and walked back to the counter. "Why?"

Kip's cell phone buzzed, but I ignored it. "A while back I found out that she was killed in a, uh, suspicious way. But no one really knows how." At least they wouldn't tell me.

"What did the investigation turn up?"

I shrugged. "All I know is she died ten or eleven years ago in a building that blew up in downtown L.A. I found some articles on Google, but I can't get any more information since I'm not a lawyer or a cop or whatever." Kip's cell buzzed again.

"And you thought I could find something?"

I offered my cheesiest smile, as if his turning me down wouldn't matter. I was such a liar. "I don't know. Maybe." Please, say *yes*; please, say *yes*.

Mr. Johnson reached into his shirt pocket and handed me a card. "Email me what you've got, and I'll see what I can do. No promises, though."

"Stupid spellcaster!" Kip yelled from the living room.

I took the card and smiled. "Thanks, Mr. Johnson."

"*Doug*," Mr. Johnson said as he disappeared down the hallway.

"Right." The cell phone buzzed again. Come on! What did the girl want? I scrolled through the texts: *sper cute cheeta sk8 shoes; pink and blue; i'll wear 2moro*

I texted: *Can't wait.*

And I wanted a girlfriend? Seemed like a whole lot of nothing. But I doubted Beth would ever text me about shoes. I returned to the couch and my bag of chips. "Your girlfriend got new shoes, and your dad has a date with a Victoria Secret model." Though I didn't know what a model would see in a half-bald dude with a moustache. Must be the uniform. Or the gun.

"You have to work too hard for your kills in this game," Kip said.

"That's what makes it fun." Which was great in a video game, but in real life . . . I hoped Mr. Johnson would help me figure out what happened to my mom. Because if he couldn't, I'd probably never find out. The Mission League liked keeping secrets.

• • •

Thursday morning in The Barn—which was the basement classroom where us agents-in-training learned our secret skills—I sat scrunching my face in concentration.

A loud click drew my gaze away from the puzzle in my hands. Gabe waved his open padlock and flashed his metal grin.

"Goody for you," I said. My stupid paperclip got stuck every time I tried to turn it inside my padlock. As usual, it was far too early for this kind of brain activity.

Besides, all I could think about was how basketball tryouts started after school today.

"Let me see it." Jensina held out her hand, her long fingernails painted electric blue to match her pixie hair. I wondered if she dyed it herself or if she'd gone to Lukas at *Peluqueria Rodriguez*.

"No way." I forced the twisted metal back into the lock and wiggled it around. I wasn't taking help from a girl. Beth's LCT training was an exception, and enough torture for my fragile ego.

"You can't force it." Gabe pushed his glasses up his nose. "Straighten the paperclip and press it to one side against the pins. Better yet, do what I did and shimmy in through the top."

If he didn't pipe down, I'd shimmy him. I gritted my teeth and wrestled with the lock. Overall I had picked up spy trainings with incredible ease and often won first points for Alpha team. But two things gave me trouble: locks and languages.

The first week back to school, Mr. S had announced that this year's summer training mission would be in Japan. He didn't say where—and wouldn't until the new recruits joined us in the spring. But we'd already started learning Japanese in the afternoons.

Japanese was nothing like Russian.

This morning's lesson was on lock picking. The center of Alpha table was heaped with all kinds of metal: deadbolts, file cabinet locks, doorknobs, and padlocks in three sizes. Gabe and Jensina's locks all lay open. They were simply waiting on the weakest link.

That would be me.

I huffed and glanced at Gabe. "What do you mean, shimmy in the top?"

"Thirty seconds left!" Mr. S called from his desk in the corner. " 'You may delay, but time will not.' "

I dropped my padlock. It clattered to the table as I snatched up a doorknob. Maybe I'd have better luck with this one.

Jensina buried her face in her arms on the tabletop and groaned. Her negativity wasn't helping. I thrust my mangled paperclip into the keyhole.

"Done!" Beth yelled.

A cheer rose from the Diakonos table, sending a jolt of surprise through me. I looked up. All five Diakonos students had their arms in the air, waving madly at Mr. S.

He approached and surveyed their locks. "Good work. Fifty points."

Diakonos team whooped and screamed. I dropped the doorknob onto the table—paperclip sticking out—and pushed it away. "It's not fair."

"What's that, Agent Garmond?" Mr. S asked.

"We've only got three people in Alpha, and Diakonos has five."

" 'Genius not only diagnoses the situation but supplies the answers,' so said Robert Graves. Diakonos may have more people, but they opened more locks in less time. That doesn't seem unfair." Mr. S walked to his desk and wrote something down. Probably the points. Like it mattered. Alpha was so far behind on points it felt like we'd been lapped twice.

"The problem's not your team, Garmond, it's you," Nick hissed from the next table. "Even if you had twenty lock-picking experts on Alpha team, you'd still lose."

As much as Nick bugged me, he had a point. And picking a fight with pretty boy Nick Muren wouldn't earn any points for my team or myself. I was at six, and I couldn't take regular LCT until I was at one hundred. Don't laugh. I'd been at negative fifty when school started. My first two lessons with Beth hadn't gone that well, and I couldn't help but notice that the rest of the class was not bruised or limping around from the regular LCT class.

Mr. S walked to the chalkboard. "If you're without a lock picking kit, there are many common household items you can use besides a paperclip. Safety pins are great. Some other good tools, depending on the size of the lock, might be an Allen-wrench, a screwdriver . . ."

I slouched in my seat and glanced at Beth at the Diakonos table. She was leaning forward taking notes. Her brown ponytail draped over her ear. I sighed and grabbed my pen.

She had better start teaching me something concrete soon.

• • •

Tryouts for basketball were after school on Thursday and Friday and almost all Saturday. Varsity coach, Martin Van Buren, thrived on making us feel like we were on the edge of being cut. He never played favorites. I'd played varsity last year as the only freshman on the team, so I felt confident, but I wanted to be the starting point guard. I'd take shooting guard, if I had to, but I was a floor general, a leader. I had the handles and the vision.

Saturday, Coach began the morning with killers. Typical. It was his way of weeding out sloths and finding players who could perform when they were dead tired. Killers consisted of running from the base line to the free throw line and back to the base line, then to half court and back to the base line, then to the far free throw line and back to the base line, then to the opposite baseline and back.

That was one.

After the third set of killers, my ankle grew tender. I was glad I'd wrapped it. I pushed harder, finished my killer, and strolled to the drinking fountain. Out of the corner of my eye, I watched those still running. All freshmen—and one junior. Desh Corneilussen, of course. He was a heavyweight varsity wrestler with more flab than muscle, but he'd likely be our center since Garcia had graduated.

I walked away from the drinking fountain and leaned against the mat-covered wall beside Kip. Now Desh was the only one still running. "The dude needs to cut out the Hot Pockets," I said.

Kip's lips twisted into a smirk. "Ain't going to happen. Desh eats pizza for breakfast, lunch, and dinner."

Next, Coach had us shoot free throws. Cake. I never missed free throws. Another *must* for a good point guard since we drew so many fouls.

After free throws, Coach picked ten random players to scrimmage. I tried not to smile when Coach threw me the ball. There were all kinds on the court—freshman to seniors—with all kinds of ability. Now wasn't the time to get cocky.

I dribbled and passed, analyzing those on my team and quickly weeding out the skilled from the unskilled.

Only a year separated me from the freshmen, but that made a huge difference. I smiled at how flustered they were around Coach, taking every comment personally. I knew better. Let the criticism bounce.

Overall, I played well, but I kept tripping over my feet under the key. It had been too long since I'd scrimmaged with real players. Plus, I'd grown over the summer—at least my feet had. I'd measured my height twice last week and got six foot, three both times.

But I was only fifteen. I couldn't be done growing yet.

Whenever someone missed a shot or didn't catch the ball, Coach made the whole team run. A gangly, butterfingered freshman was incapable of catching a pass. I even tried throwing softer. Eventually I stopped passing him the ball. My game couldn't take any more of his blunders.

Finally, Coach lined us up along the baseline and paced in front like a drill sergeant. "No practice Sunday, so enjoy your last day of freedom. Monday, practice starts after school at 2:45. Junior varsity meet with Coach Scott, varsity with me. Don't be late or you'll be running stairs. The following week we'll practice at 5:00. We've got to share the gym with the girls, so practice times alternate every other week. *Comprende?*"

A few guys murmured an affirmative response.

"Houston, Swift, Kelley, Estes, Garmond, Higgens, Frasier, Lamb, Johnson, and Corneliussen. Varsity. Everyone else, JV. If I find any talent over the next few weeks, I may pick a few swing players. Now, get lost!"

I smiled and headed for the locker room, one step closer to the starting five. I had to talk to Mr. S about the practice schedule. Hopefully he'd understand when I missed afternoon League quite a bit over the next few months.

In the locker room, I sat on the concrete bench next to Desh and untied my sneakers. Kip unlatched the locker next to me and flung it open with a loud clang. I compared my upper arm strength with Kip's. My biceps were bigger, plus Kip had yet to learn how to work his triceps.

Thank you Mr. Daggett for selling me your old weight bench.

"Got a date yet?" Kip asked, throwing a towel over his shoulder.

"You asking me out?"

Kip slammed his locker and turned to me. "For the dance, moron. You *have* to go."

I groaned. "Come on. It's stupid."

"Everyone goes to homecoming," Desh said. He rolled his hugeness off the bench and slouched toward the showers.

I stood and twisted the combination on my locker. How long would it take me to pick it with a paperclip? Ten, twelve hours?

Kip hovered beside me like a shadow. "Dude. It's homecoming."

"So? Homecoming is about football, and our team sucks. I see no reason to celebrate that." Plus, getting all dressed up to stand in the dark cafeteria, waiting all night for eight slow songs and trying to decide which girl to ask? Sounded like torture.

"Forget football. We go to the dance, then we par-tay." Kip leaned in and lowered his voice. "Get a date and you won't have to worry about who to dance with."

I glanced around, hoping no one had heard that. Kip was the only person who knew about my dance phobias.

"You and your date can ride with me and Meagan in the Bimmer."

Kip and his Bimmer. I couldn't wait 'til I got my license. But I'd need a car. I couldn't drive Grandma's Lincoln around. The thing stank like her lilac powder.

Seriously. Who'd go with me to Homecoming? Obviously not Trella-the-troll Myers.

I knew who I *wanted* to ask. But Beth was a senior and I was a sophomore, though that might not matter so much since she was homeschooled. Still, it was too early to make a play for Beth. I'd only had two LCT lessons. And I didn't want to spoil my chances because of a stupid dance.

But Kip was still hovering, so I said, "I'll think about it."

REPORT NUMBER: 4

REPORT TITLE: Some Random Prophecy Gets Me a Cell
Phone . . . and a Diary
SUBMITTED BY: Agent-in-Training Spencer Garmond
LOCATION: Harris Hall, The Barn, Pilot Point Christian
School, Pilot Point, California
DATE AND TIME: Monday, October 20, 7:36 a.m.

THE SOUNDS OF THE JAPANESE ALPHABET were so
repetitive, it was nearly impossible to pronounce wrong. Plus
Hirigana and Katakana were much easier to learn than Cryllic
had been last year. Kanji wasn't going to happen though. Mr. S
said many Japanese kids couldn't even read kanji.

I was starting to think I might actually get the hang of this
one.

"*Watashi wa* Spencer *san desu*," I said to Arianna. My
name is Spencer.

"*Konnichiwa* Spencer *chan*." Hi, Spencer . . .

Wait. *Chan*? I frowned and looked at my textbook. "Why
did you say *chan*?"

"*San* means mister or mistress, but *chan* is for close friends."

Handy that Mission-Ari Sloan was already fluent in Japanese. Maybe she'd come in useful this summer instead of driving me nuts with her mission to get me saved.

After Mr. S dismissed us Monday morning, I approached his desk. "Uh, Mr. S? Basketball practice start today after school—only every other week because we rotate with the girls' team, but . . ."

"You'll be missing afternoon class every other week?"

"Uh . . . yeah."

"You can't be two places at once, Spencer. The fact that you're asking me, tells me you've already decided."

I felt like gum on the bottom of someone's shoe.

"It's all right," Mr. S said. " 'If you can find a path with no obstacles, it probably doesn't lead anywhere.' We'll work it out. Gabe can give you your assignments. When does the season end?"

I gulped. "First week of February."

"You'll be very busy. No time for goofing off."

"Right."

"So we won't see you this afternoon, then?"

"I guess not."

"Well, have a nice practice."

"Thanks, Mr. S."

"Sure."

I dragged my sneakers across the dewy field. Which was more important? The Mission League or basketball? Last year I would've laughed at myself for even asking the question.

Now, I didn't know.

• • •

At practice that afternoon, Coach used me as point guard to teach the team the plays. A very good sign. I passed the ball to Alex Houston under the hoop, but Alex missed.

Coach threw his hands in the air. "Oh, come on, Houston!"

The team waited while Alex chased down the ball. I glanced at the clock—3:34. It felt strange to be in the gym when the rest of the agents-in-training were learning Japanese. I wondered if Beth had noticed I wasn't there.

"Hey, Garmond!" Kip hissed.

Kip and Desh waltzed through the key. It looked like they were both trying to lead.

I propped my hand on my hip. "Glad to see someone found a date for homecoming."

Their antics had worked, though, and I dwelled on my lack of prospects the rest of practice. I thought about it again that evening sitting on the mat floor of C Camp with Beth.

She started each session with ten minutes of quiet stretching and prayer. I always *tried* to pray, but my mind usually trailed off into strange places. Today I was thinking about my lack of a date for the homecoming dance. I opened my eyes, moved into a hamstring stretch, and watched Beth. I just had to man up and ask her.

Next time.

• • •

When I got home from LCT, Kimbal and Prière were sitting in the living room with Grandma Alice. Prière was the Intercessor for the Agent Development Program of the Mission League in

Pilot Point. Gabe said the guy spent more time on his face in prayer than on his back asleep.

"I hope you're here because you have some answers for me," I said to Prière, dropping my backpack and basketball on the floor under the wall of fame, which was Grandma's collection of framed pictures of old rock stars.

"*Spencer.*"

Grandma didn't like my tone, I know, but come on. It had been two and a half months since Moscow and a week since the salon incident. These people hadn't told me squat.

Prière got up from the couch and reached out to shake hands. "Bonjour, Spence. How is your training coming along?" he asked in his phlegmy French accent.

I shook his hand. "I made the team."

I think Prière frowned, but it was hard to tell with his thick moustache. "Team?"

"Basketball, right," Kimbal said. "Forgot tryouts ended on Saturday. Van Buren going to start you?"

"Too early to tell," I said. "But I'm on varsity."

"That's great, Spencer," Kimbal said. "Way to go."

"*Oui, félicitations*, Spence." Prière eased back onto the sofa and clasped his hands.

I pulled out the chair at Grandma's sewing machine and sat down, never breaking eye contact with Prière. Come on, French man, give me something I can use.

"I know that you have been waiting a very long time for answers," Prière said. "I can be providing you some of those today."

I took a deep breath. It was about time.

"Because of what happened with your parents years ago, the Mission League moved you and your grandmother into their witness relocation program and put you under surveillance. This you already know, oui?"

I nodded. My dad had done something to betray the Mission League and was responsible for my mom's death. It was the main reason I joined up, to find out what had happened. "My real first name is Jonas."

"Correct," Prière said. "Partly we were concerned about your father trying to take you or cause you harm, but there was another reason for the relocation and surveillance. A prophecy."

Whaaat? I couldn't help myself. "I'm supposed to kill Voldemort?"

Everyone stared. Crickets. As usual, my sarcasm was wasted with this crowd.

"He is joking with me again, oui?" Prière asked Kimbal.

"Yes. Spencer, zip your lip long enough for Prière to get this out, will you?" Kimbal said. "I thought you wanted to know what was going on?"

"Sorry." Sheesh. *I* thought it was funny.

"Because of this prophecy, International has been watching fourteen young men who are currently between the ages of thirteen and nineteen. These young men all match the profile of the one who will be the emissary of the prophecy. You are one of those fourteen."

So many questions popped into my head, but I kept it to two. "How do you know this? And what's that mean: emissary?"

Prière leaned back on the sofa. "To be an emissary of a prophecy is to be the one to carry it, to eventually speak it. And you match many of the elements derived from communiqués prophesied by intercessors over the last sixty years. The biggest two are that the match is male and that he is a descendent of Freidrich Lange, your great grandfather.

"Seriously?" Freidrich Lange was one of the founders of the Mission League. "Pasha asked me that in Moscow—if I was related to Lange. Anya told him to ask me."

"Precisely our concern," Kimbal said. "We think she was trying to discover whether or not you're the profile match."

I looked at Grandma, sitting quietly on her chair. She seemed awfully calm. "But what made her think I might be?"

"We have some theories, but we don't know for certain. Meeting Anya and going to Bratva headquarters was a move many interpreted as a sign," Prière said. "Perhaps they think, since you came after them, it proved you're the one."

I shifted on the sewing machine chair. "And what's the prophecy supposed to say?"

"If we knew that exactly, you would not be in danger," Prière said.

"But Anya knows?"

Kimbal leaned forward and clasped his hands. "We don't know what Anya knows."

"But I have, like, thirteen cousins who also might be it?"

"Second cousins . . . second cousins once removed," Kimbal said. "You have no first cousins since I don't have kids and your mom was an only child."

"But the bad guys want to kill me?"

"I didn't say that," Kimbal said. "The profile match is going to cause problems for a lot of people. If they can wipe the emissary out before that happens, they will. If they can turn him around to benefit their interests, they will."

Turn me. Like they turned my dad. I slouched a bit, not thrilled with Kimbal's iffy outcomes. "What about the guy in the Range Rover? Does he work for Anya?"

Prière removed his glasses, pulled out a white handkerchief from the breast pocket of his suit, and rubbed it over his lenses. "We don't know, but the fact that he approached you and called you by name leads us to believe he is connected to Anya's employer. If not, we could have a traitor in our organization."

Another traitor. Great.

Prière put his glasses back on. "After your experiences in Moscow, my superiors were adamant that you be watched even more closely than before—for your own protection and for the potential fulfillment of this prophecy. But now the international board would like to relocate you and Alice, give you new identities, and set in place two agents who would pose as your parents to throw off any suspicion."

Move? I jumped to my feet. "No way!"

"It doesn't have to be forever," Grandma said. "Just until you make this prophecy or someone else does."

"Or you outgrow the prophecy," Prière said. "Turn twenty."

"I'm not hiding until I'm twenty. I just made varsity. Please. Don't do this. Kimbal can drive me everywhere. And I promise not to take off my necklace. Ever."

"The international board has left the choice in my hands," Prière said.

So it wasn't decided yet. "Prière, please." I crossed the living room and stood in front of him, looking down. "I'll do anything you say. I'll be good. I won't talk to strangers. I won't run off on my own."

"You must promise to abide by my rules."

"I will. Anything." I would wax Prière moustache every day, if that's what it took.

"We will put cameras at this house and at your school. I will start training you in how to track your prophecies, and you must work hard to do it right."

"Why not come to dinner tomorrow night and start then?" Grandma said.

I held my breath, dreading the idea of pork chops with Prière.

"Thank you, Alice, that would be most convenient." He turned back to me. "We will also get you a cellular phone that you must carry at all times. It will have programmed emergency phone numbers. And you must wear the tracker, even during your basket-balling games."

"I get a cell phone?" I glanced at Grandma, who was scowling my way. Sweet!

"We will give this one chance, Spence," Prière said. "If I have reason to believe that we cannot keep you safe, you and Alice will have to move to a new location."

"Thank you," I said, my heart rate slowing now that the rug hadn't been fully yanked out from under my life. I *had* to stay safe. *Had* to make this work. For basketball. For Kip. For Beth.

That night I made my own emergency field ops kit. It was nice that all these spy guys were going to follow me, but I had to be able to take care of myself. LCT training and field ops kits were the best I could come up with.

I found a razor blade in a little cardboard sleeve in Grandma's bathroom. She used them to clean glass. I slid it into an unused credit card slot in my wallet. I also hid a safety pin and paperclip in some other slots in my wallet, hoping I'd never need to pick a lock.

I unwrapped a stick of gum and tucked another razor blade, safety pin, and paperclip inside the wrapper. The razor blade was too wide, so I taped the wrapper closed, hoping no one would examine it too closely. I made five gum kits and put one in each of my jackets.

Those loony boys could come and get me, 'cause I was ready.

• • •

The next night I sat at the kitchen table with Prière while Grandma Alice bustled about making some sort of casserole for dinner. Prière's people had been to the house today and installed cameras outside and in Grandma's car.

He also gave me an iPhone—an iPhone!—but the glorious new toy was sitting on my bed as Grandma had just yelled at me for playing with it when I should have been memorizing Prière's every word.

I admit, it had been hard to focus with *my precious* in my hand. Even now it was calling to me. I couldn't wait to text Kip. But I had to pay attention to Prière. My life in Pilot Point—and perhaps in general—depended on it.

"There are three methods of receiving prophecy: messengers, dreams, and glimpses," Prière said. "Messengers are extremely rare. This is when God sends an angel with a message to deliver. From what I understand, the homeless man Viktor acted as a messenger of sorts to you in Moscow, although I don't think you realized it at the time."

Yeah . . . I still wasn't convinced that Viktor was human. Isaac had thought he was an angel, which I suppose would fit with what Prière was telling me.

Viktor had wanted me to pray, something I had tried in Moscow. Maybe I should try that again sometime when I wasn't around Beth.

"Dreams happen when you are sleeping," Prière said. "Glimpses happen when you are awake. Are you keeping an intercession journal?"

"A what?"

"I will take that response as a *no*." Prière reached under the table, lifted his briefcase to his lap, and clicked it open. He pulled out a leather book that had a thin strap wrapped around the center and handed it to me.

"I'm supposed to keep a diary?"

"This will be a record of your prophetic revelations."

"A dream diary?"

Prière smoothed one side of his moustache. "If that helps you understand."

I wrinkled my nose. At least it didn't have one of those kiddy locks and keys.

"One thing you must always remember, Spence. Your journal is for you alone. It is confidential. Only you must decide what is to be reported." Prière withdrew another leather journal, this one thin and cracked with age. He flipped through the pages. "Here is one that is safe to share—and mostly in *Anglais*, which I do not often write in." He set the journal on the table and turned it so that it faced me. "Read this entry, if you please. *Rêve* is meaning 'dream.' "

I read a little chart scrawled in fresh black ink:

Date	Type	Concerning	Description
Sept 4	Glimpse	Rob Taylor, Pilot Point Unit Retiree	possible injury at construction site—check support beam
Sept 4	*Rêve*	Unknown female teen	is/will be suffering abuse
Sept 5	Glimpse	Patrick Stopplecamp, Pilot Point Unit Teacher	one of daughters—prophesies
Sept 5	Glimpse	Elizabeth Watkins, Pilot Point Unit Student	LCT *tutorat* Spencer Garmond *sans autorisation*.
Oct 4	*Rêve*	Gustov, Dresden FO contact	will refuse to held the Dresden Field Office in regards to locating his missing father.
Oct 5	*Rêve*	Unknown female teen, Asian?/Hindu? & Nicolas Muren, Pilot Point Unit Student	girl is not to be trusted— issue warning
*Oct 6	Glimpse	Prière, Pilot Point Intercessor	will get food poisoning from the cod at Jean Carlo's Bistro. Order the pasta.
Oct 6	Glimpse	Jacob Lindley, Pilot Point Unit Student	may be arrested for breaking curfew while trying to help his sister, Kathryn—issue warning.
Oct 7	Glimpse	Helene Aider, Pilot Point Unit Retiree & Jennifer Aider, Anaheim Unit Student	Jennifer might leak *confidentiel* information—issue warning to both to take care.

I gaped at the page. Some of the entries involved people I knew. One of Gabe's sisters, something in French about me and Beth and LCT—had she fibbed about being allowed to train me? Some mysterious girl and Nick. And Jake arrested? How could that be? The guy was a Boy Scout.

I turned the page.

"*Mais non.*" Prière snatched back the journal. "This is not entertainment reading, Spence. Never let anyone see your journal unless there is reason, like showing a superior an unreported entry or showing me, since I am training you. *Me comprends-tu?* Do you understand?"

"Yeah. Sorry."

"And you are not to be speaking a word of anything you saw in my journal. Is this clear?"

"Crystal."

"Now, I write up all of my prophecies in official reports, so there is no reason to ever let anyone see my journal. But occasionally there is a prophecy I do not write up, for instance the glimpse of food poisoning. That is why I put an asterisk beside the date. However, if I started to have prophecies that someone was trying to kill me, maybe I would begin wondering about the glimpse of Jean Carlo's Bistro. Perhaps there was more to that glimpse than I originally thought, oui? In that case I would go back through my journal, find this entry, and write up a report for the dream and cross out the asterisk. Is this clear?"

I nodded, my mind still fumbling over the information I'd read in Prière's journal. What was going to happen to Katie Lindley?

Grandma Alice set a plate of salad in front of me and Prière.

"*Merci*, Alice," Prière said smiling up at Grandma.

"*Tu seras toujours la bienvenue mon cher.*" Grandma smiled and waltzed back to the stove.

I shuddered. Grandma flirting in French? Wrong on so many levels.

Prière turned back to me. "Notice that dreams are often quite vague. Sometimes I do not know whom or what they are about. I log the most concrete information possible. Another thing, glimpses, they mostly occur when you are in the presence of the subject. If I remember correctly, this was true for the glimpses you reported having in Moscow. You were with the person when the glimpse occurred, yes?"

"Yeah." Most the time. I thought.

"So you see how that works. Sometimes a field agent gifted in prophecy will go undercover, hoping to receive a glimpse of a target. Although we can never force what God will show us, do you see how this could be helpful during an investigation?"

"Sure."

Grandma set a plate of bread and the butter dish between us.

"You have been using your glimpses to avoid trouble," Prière said. "That is good. It is what I did with the fish at Jean Carlo's Bistro. I do the same when I issue warnings to those on my list. I would like for you to continue with this process as well. Also, you will write official reports for all of your prophecies. Hand them in to Mr. Stopplecamp. If you have a prophecy about bad cod, you may skip the report, but log it into your journal with an asterisk just in case. Sometimes, even for you and me, dreams are only regular dreams. Do you have any questions?"

"What's going to happen to Jake's sister Katie? She's in my class. And is Beth going to get in trouble for teaching me LCT?"

"*Non*, Spence. All of what you have seen in my journal, you must forget. I only showed you to teach. Knowledge can be a terrible burden. Anything you and I see is but a glimpse of what God sees. Can you imagine his burden, Spencer? To know everything about everyone?"

I looked down and counted five cherry tomatoes on my salad. I didn't want to think about what all this had to do with God. I'd never asked for any glimpses or dreams. I didn't know why God was putting me through all this. But I had to admit, I was glad to have someone explain how to deal with it.

REPORT NUMBER: 5

REPORT TITLE: I Get a Bunch of Girls' Numbers and Strike
Out with the Prude Patrol
SUBMITTED BY: Agent-in-Training Spencer Garmond
LOCATION: Grandma Alice's House, Pilot Point, California
DATE AND TIME: Saturday, October 25, 2:00 p.m.

OUR FIRST GAME WAS LOCAL. PILOT POINT HIGH was
sort of our rival because we were the only two high schools in
town. But they were a huge school and not in our division, so
the game didn't matter for playoffs as much as for pride.

Most the Mission League kids showed up to cheer me on.
Gabe, Arianna, Isabel, Beth, Jake, and Jensina all sat two rows
behind our bench. Kip's girlfriend Megan, her best friend
Trella-the-troll, and Jake's sister, Katie, sat with them. The
girls' team had lost big to Pilot Point High in the game before
ours. Meagan had her phone out, texting a novel to some
unlucky sap. I hoped Kip knew better than to text from the
bench.

I spotted Sasquatch, Gardener, and Kimbal in the crowd. Since I couldn't wear jewelry in a game, I'd taped the charm of my cross necklace around my wrist. Had to be paranoid if I was going to keep my digs in Pilot Point.

Coach made me co-captain with Wyatt Estes, the only starting senior. Another plus. Someday, if all went well, I'd be on a college team, and later, NBA.

That was the dream, anyway.

Once some PPH kid had swept the court, I ran a baseline jump shot drill with my team to start our warm up. I glanced in Beth's direction more times than necessary, wondering if she was watching me. She was wearing her, "Don't let pink fool you" T-shirt. I loved that one.

A ball whacked me in the arm.

"Head out of the clouds, Garmond!" Coach yelled from under the key.

Nuts. I grabbed up the ball, fired it to Kip at the free throw line, then ran to the baseline. Kip passed the ball back and I shot a three-pointer. All net.

I jogged to collect the ball and whipped a pass to Alex who was next in line.

I had to get my head in the game. If I didn't pay attention, I could lose my place as a starter.

The Pilot Point Bulldogs were all juniors and seniors. With three thousand kids in the high school, they could afford to be picky. They got the jump ball, but missed their first shot. Desh rebounded and passed to me. I brought the ball down, surveying the bodies waiting at the other end. Our red and whites fought to stay in front of the blues. My ankle felt good. I'd wrapped it before the game when I'd taped my necklace to my wrist.

I held up my hand, signaled a three. It seemed the best choice considering Burbank's height. I wasn't likely to get too many passes inside their zone. Not yet, anyway.

Desh must not have seen me call the play because he was fighting for position with the Bulldog's center. Kip popped back out on my right, and I passed him the ball. He took a terrible shot that bricked off the rim. I darted in for the rebound and grabbed the ball in the air. So did Bulldog number forty-four. The power forward came down on my ankle. I screamed as I ripped the ball away. The whistle blew and the ref called a jump ball. Ours because of alternating possession.

"Good hustle, Tiger!" Beth yelled.

I smiled as we lined up for an inbounds play. Kip slapped the ball; we broke. Defense was always obsessed with the key when someone inbounded under the basket. I popped out on the baseline, Kip shot me the ball, and I sank a three. So pretty.

And the first points were ours.

After that, every time I touched the ball, I got doubled. That was fine. I wasn't the only shooter on our team. But sharp pain had begun to stab through my ankle. Forty-four had killed it. I should have asked to sit out, put some ice on it.

But this was the first game of the season, and I was playing well.

I recalled a Bible verse from Sunday school. "First pride, then the crash—the bigger the ego, the harder the fall."

Yeah . . . but this wasn't pride so much as confidence.

Burbank missed another shot. Desh rebounded and passed it to me. I moved slowly down the court, hoping it looked like I was observing and waiting for the perfect play rather than nursing an injury. I passed off to Kip and set a screen for Desh, who lumbered to the free throw line. Kip passed to Desh, but Burbank was in his face. He pitched the ball back out to Kip who passed to me. I faked, dribbled around the Bulldog, and passed to Desh for an easy dunk.

Our fans went wild. I grinned and knocked fists with Desh as we jogged back to the Burbank end.

Thirteen brought the ball down and passed left. His teammate passed it back, but I intercepted. I fast-breaked for an easy layup. But when I came down, I hopped on my right foot to avoid putting pressure on my left.

The buzzer rang and I knew. Coach had seen. I gritted my teeth and headed for the sidelines. I slapped Chaz's hand as he went in to replace me and limped to the bench.

Coach ignored me. Had to make his point. The team scooted down and made room for me in front, but Assistant Coach Scott motioned me to the end where he could look at my ankle. I sat at the end of the line and accepted a water bottle from Brent, our manager.

Coach Scott knelt beside me with an ice pack. "What's up?"

"Killed my ankle." I swung my leg up onto the bench. "Forty four came down on it."

"I saw that. If it hurt you, why didn't you come out?" Coach Scott unlaced my sneaker and pulled off my sock. My ankle was pink and swollen. I scowled out at the court. Mother puss bucket!

Coach Scott squeezed my ankle, rotated it a bit, and kept an eye on my face to gauge the pain. I wasn't giving anything away. I watched Chaz bring down the ball and throw it to Bulldog thirteen, who scored on the fast break.

"Oh, come on!" Coach screamed.

Freezing cold made me jump and look back to my foot. Coach Scott was holding the ice pack on my ankle.

Beth crouched beside us, and I forgot about the game. "You out?" she asked.

"For today he is," Coach Scott said.

"Just wrap it. I'll be fine," I said, for Beth's benefit, knowing Coach wouldn't put me back in.

"It was wrapped and you aren't fine," Coach Scott said.

"Is this the same one we munched that first day of LCT?" Beth asked me.

"Yeah."

She wrinkled her nose. "That stinks. It hasn't been bothering you all this time, has it? Because it would be stupid to work out on a bum ankle."

"It's been fine," I lied.

Beth whacked my shoulder. "Monday we'll do some therapy on it and work the ground bag, okay? Come a half hour early and soak it in the hot tub."

"Okay." That lightened my mood. Beth was going to help me. In a hot tub. I yanked back the reins of my imagination and tried to think seriously. Maybe Beth knew how to make my ankle strong again. If I'd told her it had been bothering me, this might never have happened.

The game was tied at thirty-seven when the buzzer sounded for half time. We should have been fifteen points ahead, by my count. Too many missed shots. I limped into the locker room and braced myself for a round with Coach Van Buren. We were playing rotten, and Coach lived for moments like these. Even if we were ahead by fifty, Coach would find some reason to chew us out, but today he didn't need to be creative.

Coach spat and swore and insulted our mothers. Then he prayed and we filed back out of the locker room, heads hanging in shame. I wondered what the Prude Patrol would think of that.

"Garmond." Coach put his arm around my shoulders. "This game doesn't matter. You take it easy and let that ankle heal. We need you on the court this season, you get me?"

Wow. "Yes sir."

"Good. Don't be a hero until it's worth it."

Coach headed back toward the bench. I stood alone a moment, faced the drinking fountain and grinned. It felt good to be needed. To matter.

I joined the team on the sidelines as our Pilot Point Christian School cheerleaders finished up their halftime dance performance.

I folded my arms. No offense, but our cheerleaders were pathetic. First of all, they had to wear knee-length grandma skirts. Second, any song they danced to had to be approved by our school principal, Mr. McKaffey. Third, none of them could dance anyway. And there's nothing wrong with that; I couldn't dance, either. And that's why I never did it in front of an audience.

Because that would be stupid.

Yet there our girls were, bopping and clapping to a Disney channel song. So sad. And Trella-the-troll was out front, leading the pack like she was all that and a side of fries. Finally the music stopped and they went into a cheer.

"The lions are here, to prove that we are tough.
Anything but first, is just not enough.
Now, crowd, yell with us. Get up on your feet.

We'll yell the words. And you will repeat.
PPCS. PPCS.
Look out, step back, clear out of the way.
Pilot Point Christian School will blow you away."

Parents and friends cheered. The PPH people booed. Typical away game. Not a bad cheer, though, even if they couldn't dance. They jumped and kicked their way off the court. I grabbed a ball and limped toward the hoop.

A techno beat throbbed from the speakers. Cheerleaders in blue and white sprinted out from all sides of the gym. A girl with a blond ponytail scared the living daylights out of me, whipping my arm with her hair as she blitzed past.

The girls got to the middle of the gym and started dancing. Serious dancing. Laker Girls dancing. I backed off the court and leaned against the wall beside Kip.

Pilot Point High had three times as many cheerleaders as we did. They had cute little royal blue and white uniforms. And while our girls had bopped to Disney, these girls were rockin' their bodies to some Black Eyes Peas.

They could just take their time.

Not only could they dance, they could flip too. Cartwheels and backflips and throwing each other. The song tapered off and the girls did a cheer. I don't even know what they said, but at the end, the blond one who'd scared me off the court came running from one end of the gym. She flipped into an Olympic caliber tumbling routine, bouncing and twirling past the others, who'd formed some kind of precarious standing pyramid. The tumbling girl stopped, then flipped her way back to the middle of the pyramid thingy and landed in the splits.

Whoa.

I wondered if she had a date for homecoming.

• • •

That weekend I downloaded a bunch of free apps for my phone. I got one that made gun noises, one that changed your voice, and one that sounded like a whip to use when Meagan got all old lady on Kip. I also got a bunch of girl's cell numbers from Kip, and I used "my precious" to text them. Kip seemed to think this strategy might reveal my potential dates for homecoming. All the girls texted back, mostly to ask: "Who is this?"

But once they figured out it was me, I was surprised how many were willing to chat about nothing. I mean, most of them were my Facebook friends already but for some reason, it felt so much cooler to talk by cell phone. After the exchanges, I had at least five possibilities I was willing to ask to homecoming, who I thought might say *yes*.

But I hadn't given up on Beth yet. I still had four weeks. And it would be easier to ask someone I knew. I didn't do so well talking to pretty girls until I got to know them.

Monday morning in Harris Hall, everything backfired.

"I heard you're going to homecoming with Lexi *and* Emma," Arianna said. "How are you going to manage that when you already have a girlfriend?"

I started at her. She was wearing a floor-length red skirt that looked like it came from my grandma's closet. "What?"

"They were fighting about it after Sunday school," Gabe said. "It got kind of ugly."

Girls were fighting over me? Sweet. "I haven't asked anyone to homecoming," I said, loud enough so that Beth could hear. "And I don't have a girlfriend."

"That Kimatra girl said she was your girlfriend," Arianna said. "And Lexi said you texted her."

"I did text Lexi. I mean, I asked her if she was going. But I was just making conversation. And I don't know any girl named Kimatra." I'd remember an exotic name like that.

Arianna raised one side of her unibrow. "You also ask Emma if she was going?"

"*Yeah.*" What was the big deal?

Gabe turned back to his desk and opened his Japanese textbook. The cover slapped against the desktop, and a heavy sigh hissed out his nose.

"What?" I set my jaw. The commander of the Prude Patrol might be holding his tongue, but his body language was screaming. "Say it, Gabe. Tell me what I'm doing wrong today."

But Gabe wouldn't look at me. "It's really none of my business."

"Right. You already don't think I'm good enough for any girl in this room. You made that clear at LAX. So now I can't talk to other girls, either?"

He turned a page in his book. "None of us are good enough for anyone, Spencer."

"Just tell me." I wanted to have this out now and be done with it.

Gabe turned another page. "You're treating them like meat again."

Back when I'd had a thing for Isabel, Gabe got all in my face about it. Personally, I think he just didn't like me scamming on the girl he liked. "How did I do that?"

Gabe turned in his chair. "With your phone. It's like you threw out a half dozen fishing lines baited with questions about homecoming. Of course girls would like to go to homecoming with the basketball team captain. So they all answer you, get their hopes up, start looking at dresses. Then you keep texting them, slowly reeling them in." He glanced across the room at Beth. "But you don't want to go with any of them, do you?"

What I wanted to do was get into Gabe's LCT class and use him as a punching bag. How did he *do* that? Call me out in a way that I could do nothing but agree? I lowered my voice. "Are you some kind of mind reader?"

"He has sisters," Arianna said. "He knows how these things work."

"His sisters are kids." Two identical, curly haired dolls.

"My sisters are in seventh grade," Gabe said. "And ever since school started, boys have been calling for Mary. Every day. I don't like it."

"So you're appointing yourself as every girl's big brother?" I asked. "That's a lot of girls to watch out for."

"It's just that most girls are really sentimental, Spencer," Arianna said. "If a guy starts paying attention to a girl, texting her and stuff, that's usually a sign that he likes her. Lexi showed me all your texts. She saved them and reads them over and over. She read me a few before Sunday school started, and when Emma heard, she got mad."

"I was just making conversation!" And I hadn't texted any girl anything sentimental.

"I'll try to explain to them," Arianna said.

"I just want you to think about how you might be messing with them," Gabe said. "That's all."

"Fine." Score one for the Prude Patrol. I clearly didn't know anything about girls.

• • •

That evening, I stormed the streets of Pilot Point on my way to C Camp. Coach had made me sit on the sidelines at practice and used Chaz to run plays. And Chaz had gloated about it in the locker room, as if he was some sort of threat to take my place. I didn't like his attitude or the way he was trying to divide the team. A divided team was weak.

Which meant I couldn't afford to stay mad at Gabe, or team Alpha's points would fall into the red with my personal points. Stupid, four-eyed, loafer-wearing, Boy Scout, anyway.

To top off my fabulous day, when I got to C Camp, Beth wasn't there. After she'd told me to come a half hour early and soak my ankle in the hot tub. Not cool. Mario, C Camp's physical therapist, looked at my ankle and declared it to be a Grade II sprain. Not the worst, thankfully. He wrapped it and told me I should stay off it for at least another week.

I limped out to the open practice area and found Beth waiting. She'd dragged a six foot boxing bag to the mat and dropped it on its side. Today, her T-shirt was white with a baby chicken in the center and read, "One tough chick."

"Where you been?" I asked. "I thought you wanted me to come early?"

"Didn't you?" She tossed me a pair of sparring gloves. "I thought Mario wrapped your ankle?"

"He did. But I thought *you* were going to help."

"Mario does better than I could. How does it feel?"

"It's great," I said. "Couldn't be better."

"What's your problem, Tiger? You get de-clawed or something?"

Great. Now she was mad at me. "No. Nothing."

"Well, you're bugging me. Take it out on the bag. I'll call."

I limped over to the black leather bag and knelt down beside it.

Beth yelled. "Guard!"

I moved into the guard position and started beating the bag. The purpose of working the ground bag was to practice different hold positions and strikes on the floor. I threw everything I could think of at the bag until Beth yelled. "Side mount!"

I slid into the side mount position and slammed my elbows and knees into the tough leather. It felt good to beat on something and didn't bother my ankle at all.

Being a jerk to Beth wasn't going to win me a date to homecoming, though. I elbowed the bag again and tried to rethink my strategy.

• • •

I sprint down the streets of Pilot Point at night, looking over my shoulder every few yards. I'm wearing a fancy black suit, and my shiny shoes have no traction on the sidewalk. I've lost my precious iPhone and have no way to call for help. I need to hide, but I'm afraid if I stop, I'll die.

Behind me, tires skid across the pavement as a vehicle rounds the corner. Lights illuminate the street and stretch my shadow up the pavement, long and slender like that creepy video game psychopath.

Then for some reason I stop running. The car stops too. And all goes black.

I sat up in bed, my pulse a revving Nascar engine. My hands were trembling, but I managed to flick on my bedside lamp and reach for the journal Prière had told me to start.

• • •

Two weeks later, my LCT skills had greatly improved, but I still couldn't beat Beth on the mat. On top of my daily workout at C Camp and basketball practice, I ran a mile, and every night in my room did a hundred each of squats, push-ups, and sit-ups. But I still couldn't move as fast as Beth—think as fast—or anticipate her attacks.

Monday the tenth. Two weeks remained until the homecoming dance, and I still hadn't asked Beth or anyone else. At training she darted around me, throwing jabs and punches. I was supposed to be trying to pin her—something I'd never managed—but today it was all I could do to block her strikes. I backed up and watched her bob around on the mat. Forget this. If I could fake her out—like I did playing basketball—maybe I could get behind her for a chokehold. Or sweep out a leg.

"What are you doing over there?" Beth asked.

I crept toward her. "Thinking."

She stepped back and crouched. "Well, think faster. Your opponent would have been out of here long ago."

I darted forward and pulled back my arm, faking a punch to her temple. She raised her arms for an X block. I grabbed her right wrist with my left hand and pushed her arm across her throat, then hooked my right arm around her neck, pinning her arm between us. I tugged her right leg out from under her with my ankle and we fell to the mat with me on top. I squeezed, pressing her bicep against her throat. She tried to knee me, but couldn't reach. Her legs thrashed for a moment. Her free hand snaked up my shirt and pinched the skin on the side of my waist.

I growled without moving. That really hurt. But I had her. I *so* had her!

She continued to pinch—I was pretty sure she'd broken through the skin—but I hung on. Finally she let go and slapped my side twice.

Yes! I released her and sat back on my haunches. She remained on her back, massaging her throat, then her arm. Then she lifted her head off the mat and looked at me with one eye open. "That was awesome."

Her head fell back to the mat, and she lay there like she was dead. I'd pinned her, finally! I sat, catching my breath, thinking of other ways I could use basketball and LCT together. Maybe this was the connection I'd been hoping for. A skill I had that others didn't.

Beth still lay on the mat. Her T-shirt today was light purple and had a scowling cookie face on it and the words, "Tough cookie." I crawled over and looked down on her face. Her cheeks were flushed. Her ponytail flew out above her head, and wisps of sweaty hair clung to her cheeks and forehead. "What, I pin you once and you give up?"

Her lips twitched in a smirk, but her eyes remained closed. "I'm taking five."

I'd impressed her. And she was just lying there, looking all cute and vulnerable. She had to like me, right? Spending all this time teaching me LCT. Letting me hit her. This was as good as it might ever get. Though I was terrified, I leaned in and closed my eyes. I pressed my lips against warm flesh and a rush of heat pinged through me. I'd done it! She was like a rock, though. No reciprocation, no—

"What are you doing?"

I opened my eyes. Beth held her finger against my lips, the look on her face anything but romantic. I scrambled back to sitting, my face on fire.

She propped herself up onto one elbow, her dark eyebrows furrowed. "Not happening, Spencer."

My mouth grew nauseously moist, but I managed to utter, "Why not?"

She slouched back in a heavy sigh. "Come on! I'm trying to help you."

Got to get the whole mess out in the open. "I want you to come with me to the homecoming dance."

She chuckled, her dimples mocking me. "Sorry. But I'm going to have to say no." She offered a sympathetic smile. "I don't like anybody like that, okay? And I won't."

"How can you say you won't like anybody?"

"Because God called me to serve in Special Forces. And I don't plan to get married until I know that God is done using me in the field. *And* romance makes you weak and vulnerable."

My eyes bulged. "Married?"

"No one has *ever* kissed me, Spencer, and no one will unless God releases me from this call and sends me a husband."

"A husband?" What was up with her use of the way-past-serious words?

"I'm saving my first kiss for marriage, duface."

"Oh." Wait. "*What?*"

She scrambled to her feet and headed toward the locker rooms. "You did good today," she called as she strode away. "Talk to Mr. S about getting into Boss Schwarz's class, okay?"

"You're not going to train me anymore? Because of what I did?"

She turned, continuing backwards, and lifted both arms in the air. "Sorry."

She disappeared into the locker room. The door made a soft clump as it closed. I fell back onto the mat, lying flat on my back. I wanted to die. I couldn't believe it. I'd just screwed up everything.

Dumb fool.

My heart suddenly felt like someone had punched through my chest and squeezed the blood out of it. I closed my eyes.

So stupid.

I slapped the mat by my hips. How was I supposed to know Beth was a card carrying member of the Prude Patrol? I was lucky she hadn't beaten me into liquid form. I'd never heard of a girl saving her first kiss for marriage. It seemed psycho, but at the same time . . . cool. That about summed up Beth. Psycho and cool.

Too bad it was long past over.

REPORT NUMBER: 6

REPORT TITLE: A Game of Truth or Dare Gets Me a
Homecoming Date
SUBMITTED BY: Agent-in-Training Spencer Garmond
LOCATION: 95 Juniper Avenue, Pilot Point, California
DATE AND TIME: Tuesday, November 11, 3:00 p.m.

I AVOIDED BETH, BUT FOR ALL I KNEW, she was avoiding
me, too. And now I needed to try and get into the regular LCT
class if I was going to learn enough fighting to protect myself. I
had no idea how many personal points I had. So I asked Mr. S
after class Tuesday morning.

"Let's see . . ." He opened the points book on his desk and
flipped some pages. "Well, now . . . Spencer Garmond." He
drew his finger across the page. "Ah, here we are. One hundred
points."

I crouched to look in the book. "Are you serious?"

Mr. S closed it before I could get a peek. "Is there a
problem?"

"No." But I certainly didn't remember getting that many points in the last month. But I could finally take the real LCT. "Uh . . . thanks."

The discovery was bittersweet. Jake said Boss Schwarz was an animal.

That afternoon, I took a deep breath and walked inside C Camp. I'd never been there when it was crowded. The mats were covered with students, paired off and working on a defense drill. A beast of a man stood across the room in the corner yelling commands that sent his pupils scrambling up and down on the mat.

"Knee! . . . Sprawl! . . . Clinch! . . . 1,2,3! . . . Breakfall!. . . Stand up! . . . Elbow! . . . Circle! . . . Stand up! . . . Elbow! . . . Elbow! . . . 1,2,3! . . . Knee! . . . Knee! . . ."

The guy stood about six foot five with a grayish blonde crew cut, square jaw, and bulging arms. A camouflage tee clung to his sculpted torso. He was an inflated, intimidating version of his son, Isaac—last year's Alpha team leader.

His eyes marked me, and he glared like I was a maggot in his breakfast cereal. This was not good. Mr. S said practice started at three.

"King! Take over!"

A short, muscular guy popped out of the crowd. His hair was black, and he was so tanned he looked Hispanic despite his white boy features. He yelled out commands, "Elbow . . . Circle . . . Stand up . . . 1,2,3 . . ." but his voice had nowhere near the power of Boss Schwarz's.

Boss made his way around the perimeter of the class, gaze never leaving mine. He stopped a foot away. I wanted to inch back against the wall, but I stayed put.

Steel blue eyes—hostile versions of Isaac's—scowled at me. "This is a closed class," Boss said, his voice vibrating my bones.

"Uh . . . I'm Spencer Garmond, sir. Mr. S—er, I mean Mr. Stopplecamp told me to come."

"Class starts at fourteen forty-five, Garmond. You're late."

"Sorry, sir."

"Know what we're doing?"

"Yes, sir."

"Then get out there. King! Partner up with Garmond."

King jogged across the matt to where I stood in back, still giving commands. "Breakfall . . . 1,2,3 . . . Knee . . . Elbow—"

"Sprawl! . . ." Boss Schwarz took over. "Clinch! . . . Knee! . . . 1,2,3! . . . Elbow! . . . Circle! . . . Circle! . . . Stand up! . . . Elbow! . . . Circle! . . ."

"You go," King yelled over the stampeding rhythm of bare feet and bodies slapping the mat. I dropped to the mat and circled, blocking King's offense.

Ten minutes later, Boss Schwarz yelled, "Focus mitts!"

"I'll get them." King trotted over to a supply closet along one wall. He returned with a set of black focus mitts and a pair of fighting gloves. He tossed the mitts to me. "I'll hit first so you can learn the drill."

"Thanks." I pulled the pads onto my hands as Boss's voice broke the sound barrier again.

"Ready? One!"

King's right jab almost knocked me over. I balanced my feet and braced for—

"Two!"

Left jab. Left hook. Right backhand. Right elbow. Man, this kid could hit. I wondered where he was from.

"Three!"

Right hook. Right uppercut. Left backhand. It sounded like a machine gun was going off in the room as twenty-some leather gloves smacked mitts four times each.

"Four!"

Left hook. Left uppercut. Right backhand. I saw Beth out of the corner of my eye. She was hitting with Jake.

"One!"

My wrist twanged, and I shook it.

"Pay attention, or you'll get hurt," King said.

I gripped the pads tighter and looked back to King. "Sorry."

When my turn came, I had a hard time remembering the order and did the wrong strike half the time. But towards the end of my fifteen minutes, I was getting the hang of things. This was good. A better workout. I loved the fast paced, keep-up-or-get-out, atmosphere. I could do this. I'd get stronger, faster, smarter. I was glad things had crashed with Beth.

I was such a liar.

After class, as the crowd of students dispersed, King stuck out his hand. "Devin King from Santa Monica. I'm a senior."

I shook his hand. "Spencer Garmond from here. Sophomore."

King frowned. "You're good for a sophomore. You train before?"

"Here with Beth since September."

"Watkins?" King's face puckered. "I don't know whether to laugh at you or be jealous."

I picked up my backpack from where I left it by the wall. "Laugh, King. Laugh hard."

• • •

That night in my room, I logged onto Facebook. Not only had none of the girls on my homecoming list texted me back, no one was answering my Facebook messages, either. I blamed Arianna. Her Prude Patrol "help" had likely involved warnings to stay away from the player. You know me. Scoring left and right with the ladies.

It was useless. And I wasn't going to homecoming alone, so I guessed that was that.

I logged into my gmail, just in case someone had written me there. I had over thirty messages, most of which were spam for dating services and free Viagra trials.

Not one from a real girl.

Unless . . . An email from freeforlifeservant@yahoo.com caught my eye. I clicked it open.

From: Freeforlifeservant
To: Kobefly24
Ronald Ashton's right knee still gives him trouble.
                                        –a friend

And there were three hyperlinks. The first took me to an article from the LA Times.

> LOS ANGELES—L.A.P.D detective Ronald Ashton wasn't always on the street investigating crime. Injured in December 1998 when he was shot in the knee while responding to a robbery call, Ashton took a forced extended medical leave that culminated in over two dozen

surgeries in three years. But a chance meeting with Mark Laurence, MD, a surgeon at Cedars-Sinai Medical Center, changed everything.

The article went on to say that after Ashton's knee replacement, he passed the rigorous medical review board, which allowed him to return to active duty. The second link took me to the article about the robbery when Ashton was first shot. The third link was an unrelated story about Ashton arresting a mid-list actor on a DUI charge. But there was a picture.

Ronald Ashton was Gardener, one of Kimbal's guys.

Um . . . So what? Why was someone randomly emailing me info about a member of the surveillance team? Could it be Anya, messing with me? Or perhaps it was Gardener himself, trying to make contact for some reason. Should I show the email to Kimbal or Prière?

I clicked back to my inbox to mark the spam, but I had a new email on the top of the list. It was from Kip's dad. My stomach zinged, and I opened it right away.

From: DJohnson@pppd.com
To: Kobefly24
Call my cell. 818-555-0055
Doug

I dialed the number so fast my thumb was shaking.

"Spencer, hey," Mr. Johnson said. "It wasn't easy, but I was able to get you a name. Lisa Wright. The investigation itself . . . The report is redacted, and I don't have enough clout to get the original without putting my job on the line. I only got you the name because someone owed me a favor. The article you found online said as much as the police report, though. Accidental death. Building blew up because of a gas leak."

"So you think my mom's name was Lisa Wright?"

"The woman who died was named Lisa Wright. White Caucasian, age twenty-five. The other two victims were men; I didn't ask for their names. This was the 'Explosion in Downtown L.A.' article you sent me. The other articles were dead ends. Unless you think your mom was Hispanic or you've got the wrong dates or locations."

"No, I don't think so. Thanks, Mr. Johnson."

"Glad to help. And it's *Doug*, Spencer. *Doug*."

I ended the call and Googled the name *Lisa Wright*. I finally knew my mom's name. Too common a name. A Linked In profile, a Facebook page, a CPA, and a photographer. I tried Googling her name with different versions of the words "explosion" and "died" and got nowhere. You'd think there would have been an obituary or something.

Wright could be my last name. But it could also be my mom's maiden name or another alias. I spent some time Googling "Jonas Wright" and struck out again. Arianna's comment about girls came to mind. Girls were sentimental. They saved things. Maybe Grandma Alice had kept something of my mom's. A picture. An old school assignment. Something.

Grandma kept her filing cabinet for bills and stuff in her bedroom, but she was already in bed. As busy as I'd been lately, I didn't know when I'd get a chance to snoop when she wasn't home. But a mother couldn't get rid of everything about her only child, right? I just had to find the right place.

• • •

Saturday arrived and I finally got to play ball again. My ankle didn't bother me in the game, and I was confident it had healed entirely. We creamed South Beach. I had nineteen points, fourteen assists, and nine rebounds. I was back, baby! I hated playing South Beach Christian because they had a rug gym floor. It was the only one I'd ever seen, and though I tried to be careful, I'd earned a monster rug burn on my shin when I'd gone after a loose ball. It was a battle scar, though. One I was proud of. I'd show it to Beth if she was still speaking to me.

It was an hour bus ride from South Beach to Pilot Point. The boys and girls varsity teams and the cheerleaders were all crammed on one bus. About the time we hit downtown L.A., Kip had organized a game of Truth or Dare in the back. Still sore about striking out with Beth, I wasn't in the mood for Kip's idea of entertainment. I lounged back, propping my neck on the back of the seat and my head against the cool glass, pretending to be asleep. I really *did* want to sleep—needed to sleep. Between LCT and basketball and school and my home workouts, my batteries were dead.

"Do Spencer," Kip said. "Hey, Spencer!"

I pretended not to hear, hoping he'd give up and move on to someone else. But sneakers plodded down the aisle.

"Sit down in back!" the driver yelled.

I opened my eyes in time to see Kip fall into the seat across from mine.

"Dude." He grabbed my hand and shook my arm. "You sleep more than Snow White. Is that how you keep your rose-pedal complexion?"

I pulled my arm away. "What do you want?"

"To bring you up to speed. You're about to be dared."

71

"I can't pick *truth*?" I asked.

"Not the way we're playing. It's more like *dare or dare*." Kip snorted a laugh.

I snuggled back against the window and yawned. "Sounds like *dumb or dumber*. I don't want to play."

Kip tugged my arm, pulling me away from the window. He flashed an evil grin. "Meagan is going to dare you to kiss Trella. Do a good job and then ask her to homecoming."

"You said Trella didn't want to go with me."

"Kiss her and she might change her mind."

"Oh sure." Because my kissing attempts were really working out lately.

Kip got up and walked away. "He's in, Meg. Call it."

I sat up and squinted toward the back of the bus. The cheerleaders had crowded around Desh like he was a celebrity. In the seat in front of him, Kip sat with Megan. Her lips were twisted in thought, as if the fate of the world hinged on her decision.

"Okay." She took a deep breath. "Spencer . . . you have to kiss . . . Oh, I don't know!" She burst into a fit of giggles.

"*Meg!*" Kip jerked his head at Trella and raised his eyebrows.

I wanted to die. I didn't want to kiss stupid Trella-the-troll. I looked to the front of the bus where the coaches were deep in discussion. *Hel-lo!* I wanted to yell. *A little help?*

"Meg, just say somebody!" Desh's head slumped back. "I want another turn."

"All right! Spencer has to kiss . . . Katie. On the lips."

"What!" Kip groaned. "*Meagan!*"

Everybody else cheered.

Oh, no, no, no. I mean, I liked Katie. She was cool. And cute. But Jake's sister? How was this going to make my life easier right now?

The kids in the back started to chant. "Spen-cer. Kat-ie. Spen-cer. Kat-ie."

I took a deep breath and looked around. Two seats up from mine, Katie was leaning over the back of her seat, facing me, smiling. She wore lots of smoky eye makeup, and her frizzy hair poufed in a ponytail on top of her head, like some kind of bushy tree.

I turned back to Meagan. "Maybe Katie doesn't want to play. Some girls are saving kissing for marriage." Dude. I had just sounded like the Prude Patrol.

Desh hooted with laughter. "Just take your turn, Garmond. *Today.*"

"I'm *not* saving kissing for marriage," Katie said, as if the mere idea were ridiculous.

"I know that for a fact," Kip said in a low voice.

Meagan whacked Kip in the arm and he laughed.

Yeah . . . That's what a guy likes to hear before he kisses a girl. That's she's already kissed his best friend.

Whatever. I stood and leaned over the empty seat that separated my seat from Katie's.

Everyone began to count. "One . . . two . . ."

On three, Katie and I leaned towards each other. We both made the kissing *smack*, but there was no contact. We missed completely.

I was about to give it another go, but everyone in the back of the bus cheered. I looked at Katie and she winked. Oh-kay. Guess that was that. Psychotic people, anyway.

"Okay, Okay! My turn," Desh said. "Someone dare me."

"It's Spencer's turn to dare," a girl's voice said.

"Spencer, dare me to kiss someone!" Desh said.

"I dare you to kiss Kip," I said.

"Dude, shut up. That's cheating," Desh said. "You cheat, you forfeit your turn. I say Michelle has to kiss me for one minute."

I cringed. Poor Michelle. The bus veered off the freeway. We were almost home. When we stopped at a traffic light, I relocated to the front seat by Coach Van Buren, who was talking to Coach Scott about stats. Reviewing my success in basketball soothed my pride. Because my kissing stats of late were pathetic—0 for 2.

• • •

Sasquatch had recently become a security guard at Pilot Point. He gave me a slight nod as I entered the cafeteria with Gabe to stand in the lunch line.

"I'm afraid for her, you know?" Gabe said. "I don't think he's changed as much as she thinks, but every time I say something, she gets mad at me."

"Isabel's a big girl," I said for what I felt was the hundredth time since Gabe had discovered Isabel and Nick were going to homecoming together. "She can take care of herself."

"I know. It's just that . . ."

Gabe was still talking, but when I saw Jake I tuned him out. Jake's eyebrows were so low he looked Anime angry. I shook my head. Uh oh. One ticked off big brother heading my way.

"*Jake* . . ." I said. "It was nothing. I swear."

Jake spat out a mumble of syllables and vowels that made no sense.

I held up both hands. "I didn't do anything."

Jake grabbed my arm and squeezed. "I'm hearing things, Garmond. Things I don't like hearing about you and my baby sister and a game of Truth or Dare."

Gabe stared at me.

I shook my head. "I didn't touch her." Which was true.

"Jake!" Katie raced up to the line and pulled Jake's arm. "Let go. You're hurting him!"

"Uh, no he's not," I said. Sure, Jake was squeezing my arm like some kind of tough guy, but hurting me? No.

"Calm down, baby girl," Jake said. "I'm just letting Mr. Suave know where he stands."

"He didn't do anything," Katie said. "If you would just listen—"

"Oh, I've been listening all day. Everyone saw it."

"They *thought* they saw it, but nothing happened." Katie smiled at me. "We missed."

Jake turned to Katie and leaned close. "You missed what?"

Katie sighed long and hard. "With the bus seats, we were too far away. They all counted to three and we kissed the air. Everyone cheered. End of story."

Jake's looked back to me. "You *didn't* kiss my sister?"

"Nope." I smirked at Gabe. Stick that in your juice box, Prude Patrol.

"You *missed*?" Jake released my arm and cackled. "You know, Spencer, Katie's lips aren't exactly a small target."

Katie slapped Jake's arm, and the two started yelling at each other. I continued through the line with Gabe and got my tray.

"Truth or Dare, Spencer? Really?" Gabe said.

"On the bus back from South Point," I said. "They always play."

"I thought you had a girlfriend. That one who came looking for you every afternoon a few weeks back."

"What girl?" I'd think I'd know if I had a girlfriend.

Gabe blew out a short breath and grabbed a milk. "Why do I bother?"

"You know what?" I grabbed two milks in one hand and shook them at Gabe. "Whatever." I took my tray the opposite direction of Gabe. I sat at a table with Desh and Chaz and most of the team.

"Yo, Spencer, my man!" Desh said, reaching out a fist.

I knocked it, then dove into my chicken fried steak.

"So who you taking to homecoming, dude?" Chaz asked me.

Really? There must be other things to talk about in the world. Global warming. The new Bond movie. The Lakers. "Not going," I told Chaz. All the girls that Gabe had feared I'd corrupted had found dates. And I'd blown it with Beth. There was no one left.

"You have to go," Desh said. "We're all go—"

"No, I don't. I don't have a date and I don't dance, so why get all dressed up to hang out with you people? I do that every day on the court. I prefer sweat and shorts to a zoot suit, anyway."

Chaz snickered.

"Spencer!" a girl's voice said.

I turned to the table behind me.

Katie Lindley had twisted on the bench so she could see me. "I'll go with you," she said.

Both tables fell silent. I felt the air dry my mouth. I closed it and swallowed my bite of steak.

Desh whistled. Chaz cooed like a siren. My face warmed.

"As *friends*," Katie said, her eyes flashing at Chaz and Desh.

I played it cool, acted like it didn't matter either way. I looked down at the floor, then back to Katie and shrugged. "Okay."

Desh whacked me on the back. "Well, there you go, you dog. Now you're going to have to find yourself a shower and something more than shorts."

• • •

A suit. I needed a suit. And didn't girls care about matching ties and garbage like that? Arianna said something about flowers for Katie's wrist. Why would someone put flowers on their wrist? And how were we going to get there? I couldn't drive. And I sure wasn't asking Grandma Alice to drive us. I consulted the Prude Patrol when I got to class the next morning.

Gabe laughed, obviously enjoying my naïveté. "I don't know what to tell you."

Whatever. "Well, at least I have a date." The Prude Patrol president would likely be sitting home, guarding the virtues of his twin sisters and earning merit badges.

"Maybe not." Gabe nodded behind me.

I turned my head.

Jake stood behind my chair, his expression blank. "Sup, Gabe?"

"Not much," Gabe said. "I just found out that—"

"That's great, I'm thrilled for you." Jake's hands clamped down on my shoulders, and he leaned his head close to my ear. "Garmond . . . You asked out my baby sister?"

I took a deep breath. "Yeah, that's right. You got a problem with that?"

Jake let go and sat in the chair on my right. His jaw twitched. "How you gonna get her there?"

"I have no idea."

"You'll ride with us, then. And you better buy her something nice. I don't want to see no carnation on my baby sister."

"No carnation. Got it."

"You pay for her dinner. We're going to Bella Vista. It's Italian. You eat that, right?"

"Yeah, Jake. I eat Italian."

"Right then. I'll be watching you."

"Excellent."

Jake's eyebrows jumped up on his forehead. "Don't be smart with me."

"I promise to treat her like a nun."

"Don't go and ruin all her fun, now."

I couldn't help it. I burst into laughter. Gabe too. We laughed so hard that Jake rolled his eyes and slipped away to the Diakonos table.

"You got guts," Gabe said.

I scoffed. "Jake's all talk," I said, hoping it was true.

REPORT NUMBER: 7

REPORT TITLE: I Make Out with a Tube of Tinfoil
SUBMITTED BY: Agent-in-Training Spencer Garmond
LOCATION: Grandma Alice's House, Pilot Point, California
DATE AND TIME: Saturday, April 26, 12:18 p.m.

I FINALLY BROKE DOWN AND MENTIONED the dance to Grandma. This turned out to be a good move on my part. Not only did she get me a wrist corsage for Katie, she dragged me into her room so I could see all Grandpa Earl's old suits. This could have been a disaster, but Grandma had kept everything, including some sweet suits Grandpa had worn in his twenties. I wondered if he'd ever gone undercover to some diplomatic ball like James Bond and danced with exotic foreign women.

A few of the suits had wonky huge lapels—and I wasn't touching any shirts with ruffles—but there was a descent black suit. It stank like only an old closet could, and Grandma promised to get the thing dry cleaned and the pant legs lengthened.

Donesville.

I didn't get a chance to look through the file cabinet in Grandma's bedroom, though, for pictures of my mom, but the fact that Grandma had all Grandpa Earl's old clothes seemed a good sign that she'd kept something of her daughter's too.

• • •

Jake drove a 2002 Ford Ranger. Two door. It didn't even have suicide doors. When he told me to get in the back, I just stood there holding the flower box, staring.

He couldn't be serious.

Oh, but he was. He ran around to the passenger's door and opened it so his date, Chrystal Figueroa, could get out. Jake was wearing a red bowtie to match Chrystal's red dress.

"Jake," Chrystal said, "I don't mind getting in back. Really."

"Not to worry, girl," Jake said, folding back her seat. "Spencer is a gentleman, aren't you, Spencer?"

"Sure." I just didn't know if I could fold myself up like a newspaper.

Two little jump seats folded down behind the front bucket seats. Katie already sat tucked behind Jake's seat, looking like a candy bar. Her dress was silver and shiny, and she'd piled her hair in a mountain on her head.

"Here." I reached in and handed her the flower box.

"Thanks," she said.

I stretched my left leg inside first, then dove in. My back scraped against the roof, and I curled my spine as much as possible. I reached back to make sure the seat was folded down, and sank onto it. It felt like I was sitting on a spool of thread.

"See, no problem," Jake said, pushing Chrystal's seat back into position. It hit my shoulder and knocked me against the back wall of the cab. I pulled my feet in as much as possible, hoping I wasn't stepping on Katie's.

She giggled. "Like the ride?"

"I thought clown cars were bigger on the inside."

"Don't knock my wheels," Jake said, glancing at me in the rearview mirror.

"Thanks for the corsage." Katie had opened the box and put the thing on her wrist. It was bigger than her hand.

"Nice dress," I said, which was a total lie. I would have preferred her basketball uniform over this. This normally cute girl looked like a robot dressed in aluminum ruffles.

Bella Vista was delicious. I gave Jake ten bucks more than Katie and my meals cost, determined not to give him a reason to say one thing against me come Monday.

Once we got to the dance, Jake, thankfully, ditched us. The sound was deafening in the cafeteria. Katie wrapped her silver-gloved hand around my arm and dragged me across the dance floor. I felt stupid, walking beside a tube of tinfoil.

I spotted Kip and the guys at a table in the corner, but Katie pulled me straight to the dance floor. I only stayed because it was a slow song. Slow I could do, though the moment I put my arms around Katie, the instinct came over me to pull her to the floor in a takedown hold.

She probably wouldn't have appreciated a move like that. Not like Beth would have.

On our right, a circle of onlookers was forming around two dancers. Katie took my hand and pulled us into the outer ring.

A guy twirled his date around like something out of *Dancing with the Stars.* When they came closer, I recognized

Isabel's brother Lukas—the manicure guy—and some cute blond I didn't know. He was wearing a black leather jacket over a pink shirt and gray vest, a skinny black tie, and skinny jeans. His hair was white and sculpted into a faux-hawk. His date was wearing a short white and black dress with a fat pink belt.

Man. I could appreciate the guy's style and rhythm and his date's toned legs, but did he have to make the rest of us look like chumps?

When the song ended, Katie and I went over to the basketball table. I bumped fists with the team, but before I could grab a chair, Katie kicked off her silver heels and pulled me back to the dance floor.

I just stood there, mortified, as Katie got jiggy with it. She reached out and tugged my hands a few times, as if that might trigger my groove thang.

Too bad I didn't have one.

"Hey." She pulled my head down and said into my ear, "Pretend you're holding a basketball."

I straightened, embarrassed that she was on to me and my lack of rhythm, but also intrigued by her suggestion. I closed my eyes and gave it a try. The mere idea of holding a ball instantly limbered me up. I might have looked like a freak, but at least I didn't feel like one. I was no Lukas Rodriguez, but I was okay with that.

When Katie finally got tired, she towed me to a table beside Kip's, where the girls' basketball team was sitting.

Kip came over and we bumped fists. "Saw you dancing out there. What brought that on?"

"Tell you later." Or never. Let Kip think I'd conquered my fears on my own.

"Get me some punch, Kip?" Meagan said, batting her eyes.

"Sure, babe."

As Kip walked away, I used my iPhone whip app to make the sound of a cracking whip. Kip flashed me a not-so-kind hand gesture. I laughed.

Trella leaned across the table and said, "You look hot tonight, Spencer."

Sure. Like I'd believe a word out of Trella-the-troll's mouth. But every girl at the table was staring at me, and my cheeks burned. The girls burst into giggles.

"Katie! He's blushing!" Brianna said.

Like, five of them chorused, "Awww!" in unison.

"How cute!" Michelle said.

One girl, I could maybe handle, but all of these girls at once, I admit, made me nervous. I tuned them out and used My Precious to take a picture of Kip carrying his old lady's punch back.

That was *so* going on my Facebook page.

Gabe, Arianna, Isabel, Nick, and Lukas and his hot date were dancing in a group. There were a couple other people with them. A girl named Cammy who was in my computer programming class acted like she was with Gabe. And a chubby guy who looked like he was in the chess club was standing beside Arianna. The fast song ended and a slow one came on.

"Katie, can I dance with your date?" a girl said.

"No way," Katie said. "Get your own date."

My head whipped back to the table of girls. Who'd asked that?

"Come on, please?" It was Trella-the-troll, the girl who'd said I was too tall and had ape arms. Whaaaat?

Katie hummed; her eyes rolled up at the ceiling. "Let me borrow your blue Converse?"

"Deal." Trella jumped up and grabbed my hand.

Hold up. Did Katie just trade me for a pair of Chucks? I pulled back, but Trella hung on.

Katie stuck out her bottom lip. "Please, Spencer?"

The sound of a whip turned my head to where Kip was sitting with Megan, holding up his own iPhone. Nice. He made it whip again. Well, I'd show him.

"Yeah . . . I'm a one woman man," I said, wishing Gabe had been around to hear *that*.

Trella let go of me by throwing my hand against my chest. I hadn't been ready for it, and when it slapped against my tie and Kip laughed, I felt stupid. Plus, now Katie seemed mad at me too. She and her friends went out to dance and didn't drag me along. Break my heart, I know.

I saw her say something to Jake, and wondered if she was complaining. I moved over to Kip's table, but being the only witness to their spit swapping festival turned out to be worse than sitting alone. I used My Precious to go online and post my picture of Kip on Facebook.

Jake tapped my shoulder. "I'm leaving and Katie wants to hang with her friends somewhere. You're going with her, right? So make sure she gets home."

"Uh . . . Yeah. Sure." But I didn't have a car. Did that mean I'd be stuck with Katie's friends until they took me home?

Shortly thereafter, Katie and her friends returned. She dragged me by the hand out into the hallway to a deserted corner where a gate locked off the hallway to the classrooms and lockers. She pressed up against me, the silver fabric of her dress sounded like sandpaper against my suit jacket. "You don't like Trella?"

The troll? "Not really, no."

Katie tilted her head and smirked, batting her eyes. "You know, the first time you kissed me, I saw fireworks."

My eyebrows sank. Katie's eyes flittered around my face to my hair, my eyes, my chin. Did I have something on my face? Punch?

"You're so cute," she said in a whisper, then ran her gloved fingers along the lapels of my jacket. "Don't you know?"

I shivered at her touch and shook my head. It was true. I didn't know what made girls chase after guys, but they rarely chased after me. Ape arms, perhaps? The orange hair? I didn't have a clue.

Katie giggled and leaned closer to me, looking up at my face again.

Oh. She wanted me to kiss her. I was suddenly sure of it. Only I didn't want to. This surprised me, and I fought to understand the problem. She was nice enough, but . . . well . . . she wasn't Beth.

Curse Beth Watkins, anyway. I wanted that girl out of my head.

Katie's friend Brianna interrupted my need to make a choice. "Let's go, girl."

Katie took my hand and pulled me along. I was grateful to see Chaz in the group.

"Where are we going?" I asked him.

"Cruising in the limo."

Sure enough. We all piled into a long, white limo that Chaz had rented. I ended up sandwiched between Chaz and Katie.

The car rolled forward and pulled into traffic. With ten giggling girls, it was almost louder than the dance. Chaz and I were the only guys in the car beside the driver.

Chaz opened the sunroof and we all took a turn standing out of it. It was kind of fun. But then the car stopped and everyone got out in front of a huge, two story house with pillars around the front porch. No way. I'd spent half my childhood playing here while Grandma and Nick's mom made quilts. The party was at Nick Muren's place. The parsonage.

The boom of loud music vibrated the sidewalk under my fancy shoes. Dozens of people spilled in and out the front door. Katie led me inside the dark and smoky house. The familiar smells of cigarette smoke and pot reminded me of the times the *Seis Puños*—a middle school gang Nick and I had started—had gotten into mischief here.

A few lamps were on, but the place was painted in shadows. I could hardly see the furniture through the mass of bodies dancing, sitting, standing, and—I did a double take—making out. People covered the wide staircase that curved up the side of the foyer. I didn't recognize anyone.

"Let's dance, sweet thing." A huge guy grabbed Katie and twirled her around.

She squealed and stomped on his foot, but her attempts did nothing to deter him.

"Get off!" I pulled them apart and the guy wandered away.

Katie linked her arm with mine. "Thanks."

We moved into the writhing horde. I felt queasy. Was it the cigarette smoke? No. It was something else. Something dark. Like the creepy feeling Anya or Dmitri Berkovitch gave off when I'd met them in Moscow.

"We should leave," I said. Besides, with the racket this party was making, the cops wouldn't be long, and an arrest would get me suspended from the team.

"We just got here," Katie said. "Let's look for Nick."

Yeah . . . I *so* didn't want to run into Nick Muren. "Let's not and say we did."

"Let's find someplace to sit, then."

Sit? Why?

"Here." Katie pushed me into an armchair by the fireplace and sat on my lap. Before I could say anything, she started kissing me.

Oh . . . kay.

I lost track of the time, letting the girl have her way with my lips. Maybe Kip would see us and get off my back about my not having a girlfriend. But I didn't want Katie to claim me as her boyfriend, though. That could be Sherry all over again. Even if Katie wasn't crazy—and that was a big if—I didn't want the whole ball and chain thing Kip had going with Megan. Not with Katie, anyway. She was really cute, but . . .

I grabbed her face and pushed her back. "Hey," I said.

Her eyes yawned open. "Yeah?"

"I, uh . . . I can't do this." I could, actually. I rather liked kissing girls. But as Coach always said, *"The best defense is a good offense."*

Katie's eyes clouded. "What?"

Oh, Jake was going to kill me. "I'm sorry, I . . ." I couldn't believe I almost gave her the, *"It's not you, it's me"* line. I pushed her off my lap and stood. She folded her arms, pouting. Great. "Hey, why don't we go outside?" Before the cops arrested us and I lost everything?

"Whatever." She started for the door, but Lukas Rodriquez blocked our way.

"You see my sister?" he asked me.

"Oh, hey, Lukas. No. Where's your date?" I scanned the room for the hot blond.

"By the door. She doesn't want to come in. I'm just here to get Isabel out."

"Right." Protective brother at it again. But even I didn't like the idea of Isabel at this party. "Hey, Katie. Why don't you go stand with Lukas' date at the door?"

She folded her arms and scowled. "You're not the boss of me, Spencer."

See? I did not want that snarky tone in a girlfriend. Major crisis averted. "I'm just going to help Lukas find his sister, then we'll go."

"Then *you* can go. This date is over. Do what you want." And she stalked toward the kitchen.

"Ouch," Lukas said.

"Yeah . . ." But that hadn't hurt as bad as my confrontation with Jake likely would.

"Garmond! Lose your date?" Kip and Meagan were making their way through the crowd toward me and Lukas.

"You guys seen Nick?" I asked.

"Upstairs," Kip said. "That's where they've got the good smoke."

Lukas took off.

"Thanks," I said to Kip. "Later."

I barely managed to climb the stairs, stepping over people the entire way. The second floor wasn't as crowded as downstairs, but there were still plenty of bodies. It was a little quieter, too. Lukas peeked in and out of doors, looking for Nick's room.

"It's the last one on the left," I said, remembering the cool Legos Nick used to have.

Lukas strode down the hall and went inside. I followed. Nick's room was a master suite. He had his own balcony, bathroom, TV, DVD player, and stereo. No sign of his Legos.

But Isabel was sitting at Nick's desk, playing solitaire on a massive flat screen monitor. A really, really sweet monitor.

"Lukas!" Isabel jumped up, scowling. "What are you doing here?" Her gaze landed on me. "*Hola, Es-pensor.* Is something wrong?"

"Are you crazy, Izzy?" Lukas yelled. "Do you know what's going on downstairs?"

"A party?" she said.

Lukas crossed the room and grabbed Isabel's arm, pulling her out of the chair. "We're leaving. *¡Ahora!*"

"Let go!" She jerked away from him and shoved him back. "I can take care of myself."

"*¡Mentirosa!* And I guess you can take care of yourself in jail, too, huh?" Lukas said. "People are smoking pot and getting drunk. What would Mami say?"

"You're going to tell on me? I'm not doing anything wrong."

I marched into the room and put myself between Isabel and Lukas. "Isabel, I know you don't want to think bad about Nick, but this party . . . This is a bad scene, right? I mean, this is your pastor's house, and if the cops show, they'll arrest everyone. Trust me."

Isabel's expression softened. "*Neek* only invited ten people, *Es-pensor*, but they brought friends, who brought more friends. *Neek* didn't mean for things to get out of control."

Sure he didn't. "I've known Nick a long time," I said. "This isn't his first time playing bash host." Though he'd usually kept them smaller and quieter.

"He was doing so good until his new friends . . ." Her voice cracked and tears glistened in her eyes.

"Izzy, I'll carry you out if I have to," Lukas said.

She glared at him. "You don't even know what you're doing. *¡Arruinaste todo!*"

"*¡Ahora!* We should hurry," Lukas said. "I left Grace out front, and she's not happy to be here."

Isabel gasped and pushed Lukas again. "You *tonto*. You made Grace come here?"

"*You* didn't leave me a choice."

"The poor thing." Isabel ran out the door.

Lukas and I looked at each other, then followed.

Nick appeared at the bottom of the stairs. "Baby, where are you going?"

"I'm sorry, *Neek*. I've got to go." Isabel pushed up onto her toes and kissed him on the lips. "Call me later?"

Lukas pulled his sister away from Nick and headed for the front door. I followed, hoping I might catch a ride.

"Hey, Garmond," Nick called after me. "Katie's in the kitchen. Says she really wants to talk to you."

I sighed and turned back. Guess I'd be walking home. Followed Nick down the hall, past the bathroom. Maybe I could talk Katie into leaving. If I made sure she got home, Jake couldn't be too upset, right? Plus I might not have to walk.

We passed a guy with a twelve pack, who handed me a can of beer. I walked into the kitchen and set the can on the counter. No way was I drinking when the cops would get here any moment. There were four people sitting at the kitchen bar. None of them were Katie.

Nick pointed to the sliding glass doors beyond the kitchen table. "I think she went out on the patio."

Nick being civil? At least something was going my way tonight. "Thanks, man." A chill ran over me as I crossed the kitchen. Must be getting cold out. But as I pulled the door aside, a warm breeze embraced me. I stepped out onto the patio. "Katie?"

A shadow shifted on the porch. Before I could turn to see who was behind me, cold metal pressed against the back of my neck.

REPORT NUMBER: 8

REPORT TITLE: I Get Tranked
SUBMITTED BY: Agent-in-Training Spencer Garmond
LOCATION: Nick Muren's Backyard, 1052 N. Elm Street, Pilot Point, California
DATE AND TIME: Friday, November 21, 11:04 p.m.

I SHIVERED, LIGHTHEADED AND COLD, yet hot with fear. I didn't dare move until I could remember what Beth and Coach Schwarz had taught me about guns.

Squat. We hadn't gotten that far yet.

But Mr. S had said if someone pointed a gun at you and merely threatened to shoot, they wanted something. I needed to stay calm and figure out what.

I lifted my hands. "My wallet is in my pocket."

"I don't want your wallet, kid," a familiar, smooth voice said.

Another shadow shifted. Someone grabbed my left arm and stabbed a needle into my shoulder. I cried out. Whaaaat?

I dropped into a crouch and pulled away, stumbling over the deck. I sank into a fighting stance, my shoulder burning from the needle's sting.

There were two of them. The same two who'd come after me before. The blade of grass had gone Goth. His hair, clothes, and lips were black. A thin, silver chain ran from his left ear to his nose ring. Tattoo Hulk was holding the gun, down at his side now. The fact that they were just standing there told me one thing. They were waiting for me to go down from whatever was in that injection.

I turned and ran.

"Get the car, Tito!" the blade yelled. "I'll follow him."

I leapt off the porch and sprinted over the lawn, across the street, and around the side of Cornerstone Church. I ran into the corridor between the youth building and the sanctuary and slowed to a stop. For a moment everything seemed quiet. Then the steady sound of crickets grew over the faint bass beat of the party at Nick's. I fumbled for my cell phone, but it was gone.

My Precious? Where was it? I'd taken that picture of Kip at the dance . . .

Mother puss bucket! I couldn't believe I'd lost my iPhone. I touched my necklace, hoping, at least, that Kimbal was tracking me. I should hide somewhere until he found me. Maybe go up on the roof where Nick and I used to hock loogies on cars parked in the handicap spots.

But what about the injection? I might need a doctor. What if I died here, waiting for Kimbal to show?

Footsteps in the parking lot sent me running again. I left the church property and came out on Willow. My house was six blocks from here. I poured on the speed.

Few cars were on the street at this hour, and most the traffic lights shone in my favor. I cut down a side street, taking a short cut past several apartment complexes. Headlights gleamed behind me, illuminating the street and casting my shadow long and large on the street ahead like the Slender Man. The car didn't pass, though, and I turned and jogged backwards for a moment.

Wait a minute . . . I'd dreamed this!

A vehicle was parked along the curb at the end of the block, its lights on. The streetlamp a few yards behind it cast a faint glow on the vehicle's roof. It was black. That was all I could make out with the blinding headlights, but I'd bet my missing iPhone it was a Ranger Rover. I turned and sprinted for the corner. My eyes watered in the cool night air.

I stopped at the light on Seventh and Willow, but there were no cars coming, so I ran across. Halfway down the next block, sudden fatigue overwhelmed me and I slowed to a pathetic jog. My arms and legs felt like sandbags, but my head buzzed like I'd just smoked a bowl. A streetlamp shot into the sky like a rocket, and I stopped to watch, confused.

I was still standing there, staring at the rocket when a car stopped on the road beside me. Some guy got out. An alien, I think. Massive. His face was covered in tribal markings. The rocket must have dropped him off.

"Welcome to our planet," I heard myself say.

I blinked once. Twice. The alien's lips were moving, but I couldn't hear. My eyes fluttered. Blackness tugged at the corners of my vision. Someone grabbed me. Dizziness overpowered me, and I fell.

● ● ●

I woke on the floor of a dark room, lying on my left side, my face in a puddle of my own drool. My wallet was an uncomfortable lump under my left hip, and my left arm was asleep and tingling. Techno music blared nearby. A shaft of pulsing blue light caught my attention. The light was coming from a crack under a door. It throbbed with the techno beat.

How had I'd gotten here?

I closed my eyes and tried to focus. I'd been dancing. With a blond girl with nice legs. Where had I learned to dance like Derek Hough?

Wait. That hadn't been me.

Oh, God, help. Please.

The words felt strange in my mind. It had been far too long since I'd prayed. I tried to move, but my hands were tied behind my back. My ankles were bound too. I flashed back to the initiation abduction last year.

"Not that there's a reason for anyone to abduct you simply for being a part of the Mission League," Mr. S had said.

Yeah, right.

Those guys at Nick's party had drugged me. Isabel had said something about Nick's new friends. Could she have been talking about Hulk and the blade?

I rolled to my back, then pushed onto my shoulders, working to pull my hands under my backside. The cross on my necklace slid off the side of my neck. Good. They hadn't taken it. I hoped Kimbal would get the signal and get here soon.

I tugged and strained until my hands slipped past my rear. See, Trella? Ape arms are good for basketball and contortion positions when one needs to escape from maniacal kidnappers.

I pulled my knees to my chest and threaded my feet through one at a time. And that was easier said than done. My left arm tingled like mad, and my elbows ached from the strain I'd put on my arms. I pushed up to a sitting position and felt my bonds. Rope, lots of it, tied tightly around my wrists and ankles. I felt for a knot but couldn't locate it. Forget that.

I pulled out my wallet, thankful I hadn't given it to Tattoo Hulk. After a lot of finagling, I managed to withdraw the razor blade from the little wallet pocket and the cardboard sleeve. I used the razor to saw the rope around my ankles. Cake. But my wrists . . . I tried to twist my hands so I could get a good position—man, they'd tied the rope tight. Plus I kept dropping the blade, which wasn't easy to pick up off the concrete tile floor.

I cut at that rope for three days . . . at least that's what it felt like. I kept nicking myself, or my hand would spasm from a cramp that made me drop the razor again. I sawed at the rope on the back of my left wrist, then got tired and tried the spot in front, between my wrists. When I finally broke through I cackled—silently, of course—like a madman.

Jason Bourne would have sliced through on his first try. That just went to show you how very wrong Hollywood was about these things.

I stood and my head spun. My eyes lost focus and my stomach lurched. I lunged toward the crack of light and, hopefully, the door. I felt smooth wood under my hands and held myself up until the dizziness passed.

My body felt like it was made of rubber. Whatever they'd tranked me with was heavy stuff. I felt along the door until I found the handle, paused, and continued feeling until I found a light switch. I flipped it.

The brightness blinded me at first, so I looked at the floor and blinked until I could see. I was in a supply closet, edged on three sides with floor to ceiling wire racks stocked with boxes of soda cups, napkins, trash bags, cleaners. I needed a weapon, but all I could find to hit someone with was a push broom or a mop. I picked up the broom, squeezed the handle, gave it a few practice swings, then dropped it and grabbed a can of Lysol.

Oh yeah . . . I'd go out Lukas Rodriguez style.

I got ready with the Lysol in my right hand and turned the door handle. Locked.

For a brief moment, I knew I was dead. Why did it have to be a lock? But then I took a closer look. The lock was on the outside of the door, and this was one of those privacy locksets, with the little hole. Relief showed itself in the form of excitement as I dug out a paperclip from my pocket and bent it into a straight line. I inserted it into the hole, and after a little finagling, it clicked.

I readied my Lysol again and cracked open the door. The music pulsed. The room blurred in a dark rainbow of colors and flashing lights. The shapes of dancing bodies rocked beyond a bar. The door had opened behind the counter. I could see people sitting at the bar down on my left. I'd either have to sneak along the back or go over the top.

I slipped out and shut the door behind me, pressing up against it. A curvy waitress sauntered by dressed in a sports bra and a pair of boy shorts. She carried a tray filled with drinks. She glanced at me and I her. Well, hello there, my lovely. I smiled.

"Blaine," she said without stopping, her high heels clicking on the floor. "Your boy's awake."

Traitor. I leaned out from the wall and looked both ways. A cluster of bustling bartenders were mixing drinks to my left. And to my right, the hot waitress had just slipped around the massive body of Tito, the tattooed hulk. The blade of grass, who I guessed must be Blaine, stood right in front of him.

Blaine walked toward me slowly, like he was trying to corner a cat. So I made like a cat, climbed on the shelf under the bar, and hoisted myself up onto the counter.

Blaine grabbed my leg. I turned and sprayed Lysol into his eyes. He screamed but held on, so I bashed the can against his head until he let go. I leapt off the counter and ran onto the dance floor, my shiny dress shoes sliding all over the place. Bodies quaked around me. I crouched down and wove around them, scanning where the ceiling met the walls for an exit sign.

Someone slapped my back. I spun around, but it was just some chick's scarf. I caught sight of the glowing green exit sign then, back the way I'd come. I made for it, going as fast as I could. A guy knocked into me. I tripped over my own feet and fell on my knees. I scrambled to stand, slipping on the floor.

Tito got to me first. He grabbed my necktie and dragged me over to the wall, feet from the exit. So close to freedom, but I was trapped, my necktie a leash in Tito's fist.

I dug my fingers under my tie to ease the chafing and loosen it so it could go over my head, but Tito let go and snagged my right arm, his grip the Jaws of Life.

I punched his metal abs with my free hand. Still useless. I pulled back to try again, but one of the bouncers grabbed my arm before I could swing. I kicked out but made no contact. Tito forced me to the floor on my back. The curvy waitress pushed through the men and leaned over me, which would have been nice if she hadn't been holding a syringe.

Fire shot through my every pore; my heart hammered. The waitress got down on her knees and held the syringe near my arm. I thrashed and pulled and kicked.

"Hold him still," the waitress said. "What if I break the needle?"

"Just stab it in." The tattoo of a spider on Tito's cheek seemed alive when he spoke. "Wait." He sat on me, crushing my gut. He pinned my arm to the floor at my elbow and put his other hand on my throat.

The skin to skin contact brought an instant drop in temperature. I looked into his eyes. They'd been brown before, I was sure of it, but now they were pools of blackness. Nausea reeled in my gut. My limbs started to quiver. No. Not this.

This was what had happened with Dmitri in Moscow.

This was what happened when the baddies were near.

The waitress came at me again.

"No, please. Don't," I said.

Her eyes flicked to mine. No creepy blackness there. Just concern. Good girl.

"I'm just a kid," I said, milking it. "And they took my girlfriend somewhere. What'd they do with her?"

"What?" The waitress sat back on her heels, her sculpted eyebrows furrowed in concern for my missing sweetheart. "Where is his girl?"

"Don't listen to him, Trish," someone said. "He's lying."

But Trish didn't look so sure.

A loud thump turned her head. Her eyes widened, and she got up and ran. Someone grunted, and my right arm was suddenly free. I punched Tito's ear. But he tightened his grip on my throat.

Someone yelled. "Get off!"

Tito turned to look behind him, releasing my neck. I peered over his arm and caught sight of familiar orange hair.

Kimbal?

Another man stepped into view over Tito's shoulders and looked down on me. Tall. Hairy. Sasquatch. "Let him up." The man had a twangy European accent, sort of like Prière's.

Tito released me, heaved to his feet, then pulled a knife on Sasquatch.

What a moron.

I sat up and pushed back against the wall. Over by the door, Kimbal was cuffing Blaine. Tito and Sasquatch faced each other. The techno music was still thumping, but the crowd had formed a half circle around them. Tito had fifty pounds on Sasquatch, but I'd bet money Sasquatch was wearing a bullet-proof vest.

Might not matter against a knife, though.

Tito jabbed his blade in from the side. Sasquatch held up his forearm, blocking the attack, then snagged Tito's wrist with his other hand and pulled down.

Tito crumpled, screaming every curse word in the Spanish language. Sasquatch rolled him onto his stomach and cuffed him.

Man. When Beth said subdue without harm, I hadn't believed it was possible.

Sasquatch held out his hand. "You okay?"

"I think so." I grabbed his arm, and he pulled me up.

"Let's go, Garmond." Kimbal gripped my shoulder and steered me toward the door. "I'll take you home."

The fresh air outside the club was like breathing for the first time. I hadn't realized how hot and stuffy it had been in there. I glanced over my shoulder at the building, my limbs still trembling. The word "Blaze" glowed in blue glass letters above a heavy black door.

Wait. I knew where this place was. It was just a few blocks from the mall.

Kimbal stuffed me into the back of his squad car. I let my head fall back against the hard plastic seat and closed my eyes. The trembling was almost gone, but my heart still raced in my chest. I breathed slowly, trying to calm myself. I didn't want to think about what had happened.

Kimbal took me to the hospital to get checked out. The doctor said the injection had been liquid iVitrax, aka Rose Water, some fancy new street drug that rivaled Meth.

I hadn't overdosed on it, though, and the doctor let me go home that night.

I couldn't sleep. I kept replaying the different events over in my mind. It was all so confusing, so muddled in my head. No matter how scary it had been, I always came back to Sasquatch batting Tito aside like a shower curtain. That guy was awesome.

They'd caught the bad guys. It was finally over.

REPORT NUMBER: 9

REPORT TITLE: I Get Used as Bait to Catch a Traitor
SUBMITTED BY: Agent-in-Training Spencer Garmond
LOCATION: Grandma Alice's House, Pilot Point, California
DATE AND TIME: Sunday, November 23, 2:37 p.m.

"IT'S NOT OVER." PRIÈRE SAID. "Somewhere, there is a leak."

Prière had come to see me Sunday afternoon. I'd thought he and I were going to do some intercession training, but instead he dropped this bomb. He'd also returned my iPhone. Guess who had it? Katie Lindley, the little thief.

"A traitor in the Mission League?" I asked.

"The two men who abducted you have implicated no one, but there are things that do not add up. And so I am here and no one else."

"I don't understand."

"Someone you know is helping the other side. We have questioned everyone and have not yet determined the leak."

"Easy. It's Nick." Those guys were at his house, and Nick had sent me right to them.

"I will share with you what I have discovered during the interrogations, but you must not make accusations or speak to anyone of what I say, or it could ruin our investigation. Not even Agent Kimbal or Mr. or Mrs. Stopplecamp. Me comprends-tu? Do you understand?"

What? "Kimbal and the Stopplecamps traitors? No way."

"*S'il te plait*, Spence. You must promise me, or we will relocate you immediately."

"Okay, okay. I promise."

"First of all, oui. Young Mr. Muren has made some dangerous friends. He claims to have met them at the dancing club Blaze, where we found you. He says he did not know why they wanted to meet you, but did not see any harm in arranging an introduction."

I snorted. "Sure he didn't."

"As I told you, we tracked your cellular phone to Katie Lindley. She claims Nick offered her five hundred American dollars to bring you to his home and take your phone."

Nice. So my homecoming date was a set-up. Wonderful. "Doesn't that prove it was Nick? Five hundred dollars? Why would he do that?"

"He said his friends claim that they knew you from a street gang and wanted to play a prank on you. He said it was their five hundred dollars he offered, not his."

"Yeah, right."

"We are also questioning Isabel Rodriguez, who has spent much time with Mr. Muren and learned that he has been dating a girl who was meant for you."

"I'm sorry, what? I thought Isabel was dating Nick?"

Prière shook his head. "Kimatra Patel came to Pilot Point about the time your afternoon basketball practices began. According to Isabel and her brother Lukas, she asked for you a few times outside Room 401. Then one day, Nick claimed to be you and went off with Kimatra."

"What?" I laughed. "That's crazy. What did Nick say about that?"

"If you must know, he said, 'The girl was too beautiful for Garmond.' "

What a tool. "So he stole my girl." A girl who was meant to be some kind of trap, apparently. But still. I'd like to get a look at this mystery girl. "Why was Lukas there?"

"Lukas has been following his sister of his own accord. He does not like Mr. Muren and did not care for Isabel's assignment to get close to him."

"Assignment?" That explained why Isabel was "dating" Nick. "But I didn't think we got real assignments in high school. And why does Lukas know about it?"

"Occasionally a real assignment is given. We felt that Isabel was having the best odds of finding out what Nick was doing. Though her family is not very discrete, it seems."

"If you already suspect Nick, why not arrested him?" Put the sucker behind bars.

"But for his dislike of you, we have no proof that he has done anything wrong. His explanations paint him as a mischievous and somewhat curious adolescent male but nothing more."

"Oh, come on." But I had to agree. Seriously, why would Nick go *that* low? Help some freaks kidnap me? Sure, the guy was rebelling against being a pastor's kid, and he was still ticked about my talking to the cops back in middle school, but help some creeps abduct me? I didn't know . . .

"So what now?" I asked. "And please say you're not going to make me move."

"Not yet. What I would like is for you to enter the District League Combat Training event. It is the first weekend of December."

That was two weeks away. "Uh . . . I pretty much suck at LCT."

"That is not what's important. I believe that this event could offer the very best *méthode* of catching the leak. And with so many agents present, I feel you will be very safe."

Oh. "So . . . I'm bait."

"It is sounding so negative when you are saying it in such a way, but, eh . . . oui." Prière shrugged one shoulder and gave me an innocent smile. "Bait."

Fabulous.

• • •

"Let's bridge and roll!"

It was Monday night, and I was already tired from basketball practice. I flopped down to the mat with the other advanced LCT students and tried to keep up as Boss Schwarz barked out commands.

"One! . . . Recover! . . . Two! . . . Recover! . . . Three! When someone has you in the mount position, you need to create leverage and space to allow yourself a chance to escape! Recover! . . . Four! . . . Recover! . . . One! . . ."

Nice timing. That would have been good to know last Saturday night when Tito had sat on me.

Boss Schwarz went on for fifteen minutes of bridge and roll, then switched to the knee-elbow escape drill.

"We work hard to get strong to protect ourselves on the field," Boss yelled in the middle of the knee-elbow drill. "But don't trust in your own strength. Trust in God's power over the power of human might. The same God who delivered David from Goliath can deliver us from every foe."

After warm-ups, Boss ordered us to work on escape drills with a partner.

Devin pushed me to the floor. "You first. Let's do mount."

I lay on my back, but before Devin could take position, Jake elbowed him out of the way and plopped down on my gut.

I groaned through his unexpected weight. "What are you doing?"

"You and I need to chat." Jake looked up at Devin and grinned a cheesy smile. "King, my man. Find another partner."

"Whatever." Devin slouched away.

Jake looked back to me, his jaw flexed, his brown eyes like bullets. He curled forward and locked onto my neck. "You going to try and escape, or are we just going to cuddle?"

I grabbed Jake's foot and did the bridge and roll. Jake flipped to his back on the mat with me on top in a side mount.

"Good. Good," Jake said, squirming. "I see you got the hang of this jujitsu business." Jake pulled my head down and fought for the knee-elbow leverage. I squeezed into him with all my strength, but Jake got by and slipped into the full guard position, locking his legs around my waist and still gripping my head.

I was on my knees now. I managed to free my head, then grabbed Jake's waistband and pushed, straightening my arms and popping to my feet.

"Whoa!" Jake said. "What was that move?"

"Superman."

Jake stood. "What you talking about Superman? I never learned no Superman."

"Beth taught me."

"Uh-huh." Jake snapped his fingers and pointed to the floor. "My turn, Clark Kent. On your belly, like you're flying."

I flopped onto the mat. Jake sat on me in the back mount position. "Now, I'd like to know why Superman would take the lovely Lois Lane to a party that she's not allowed to attend, then abandon her. See, I think Superman isn't so super, that's what I think."

I grappled for Jake's arm. "I apologized to Katie today at lunch." Actually, I'd sarcastically apologized and thanked her for trying to get me killed. I'd made her cry, but it had been worth it, the sneaky little kissing, cell phone thief, anyway. "You told me to go with her and her friends. That's where they went. But . . ." I grunted and managed to turn over onto my knees, stuck in Jake's guard again.

"But what?" Jake asked.

"She got mad at me when I wanted to leave. Then I . . . I couldn't find her. Why don't you get on Nick's case for throwing the party in the first place?" I so wanted to tell him that Nick had paid Katie five hundred buck to get me to that party, but Prière didn't want me talking about it.

Keeping secrets sucked. It was way easier to blab.

I grabbed Jake's waist for the Superman again, but he was wise to it now and pulled me into a headlock.

He flicked my ear. "I'm on your case because you were responsible for my baby sister, and you took her into an environment where drugs and alcohol were present."

I popped to my feet, my head still stuck in Jake's grip. "I tried to make her leave."

"You didn't try hard enough, Superman." Gravity worked, and Jake released my head. His own head dangled upside down, an inch above the mat. His legs still clutched my waist.

I pushed down on Jake's neck. He fought me for a good five seconds before he groaned and his legs burst free and hit the mat.

"Look," I said. "It's not going to work out with Katie and me. We're just friends, so you don't have anything to worry about, okay?"

"I'd better not, 'cause I'll wipe the floor with you." Jake scowled one last time before launching to his feet and skulking off to the locker room.

I took a deep breath, then laughed out loud. I'd like to see Jake try and wipe the floor with me. Jake's growl was far worse than his guard.

●　●　●

The next two weeks flew by. Despite Thanksgiving, Coach Van Buren held six practices a week. So did Boss Schwarz. And now that I had officially entered the LCT competition, I couldn't really afford to shirk practices there. Basketball practices were child's play compared to what Boss Schwarz put us through.

I didn't stop there. I spent every free hour I could in the school weight room or working the bags at the center. If I couldn't do either, I'd do my sit-ups, push-ups, squats, and body conditioning at home. I didn't want to be weak if someone came after me again. And I also didn't want to humiliate myself at LCT District, even if it was a sham. But most of all, I needed to make this work. Because if they didn't figure out who the leak was at LCT District, I'd have to move. And I couldn't let that happen.

• • •

On Friday, December 5, Kimbal drove me to a private athletic facility in Westwood where the Los Angeles District League Combat Training tournament was being held. The place had three gyms, two pools, and a bunch of other stuff like tennis and racquetball courts, exercise machines, and weight training rooms.

I found the registration table and got in the A-M line. They gave me a lanyard with my name and hometown on one side and a list of competition times on the back.

"Let me see," Kimbal said, before I got a chance to read the thing myself. "You're in Gym One in forty minutes, ring four."

I snatched the lanyard back and put it over my head as Kimbal dragged me to Gym One.

"You earn points in three areas: submission, defense, and combat," Kimbal said.

"I know."

"They award medals in each area and in overall achievement."

"Yeah, I know. Boss Schwarz told me."

"Today is just the prelims. If you make the top twenty-five in any category, you'll compete in the finals tomorrow. Oh, and make sure you listen to the announcements. Sometimes there's a change and they page you. If you hear your name, come to the registration table. Let's get you there so you can stretch and I can scan the crowd."

"Okay." The way Kimbal was going on and on, you'd think he was competing and not me. It was hard for me not to scan the crowd too, though I didn't really know who I was looking for. If there was a traitor, he or she might be a face I recognized and trusted, right?

Gym one had eight rings, which were square sections of blue mats with a red number in the middle. Each ring had a table where three judges sat. Bleachers lined the long sides of the gym. Kimbal and I claimed a spot in the center. I took off my shoes. My uniform consisted of a black rash guard short sleeved shirt, white and black knee-length MMA fight shorts, open-finger gloves, a mouth guard, and a protective cup. Bare feet.

I watched two guys fight in ring one. The guy in red had the guy in blue in back control with both arms trapped. Too bad for blue.

I couldn't believe I'd agreed to this. I so didn't feel qualified to fight in a tournament.

The first familiar face I saw was Isaac Schwarz, Boss Schwarz's son and the guy who'd been assigned to keep an eye on me in Moscow. He was refereeing the match at ring four, wearing the same black pants, polo, and latex gloves the other refs wore. Isaac used to wear T-shirts, shorts, and flip flops, and his shaggy hair had always hung past his eyes. It was weird to see him in all black with a buzz cut.

When his match ended, he came over to where I was stretching on the floor.

"Look at you, my little apprentice. Making district. I'm so proud."

If he only knew. "Nice hair."

"Yeah . . . everybody gets the buzz at Mount Awful."

"What's with the gloves?"

Isaac peeled them off and tossed them in a trash can by the judges' table. "That's so I don't have to touch your nasty blood and sweat when I pull your opponent off you."

Swell.

Another ref passed by and Isaac grabbed his arm. "Tony, Meet Spencer Garmond. Spencer, Tony is one of Beth's big brothers. He used to be in Alpha team when he was at Pilot Point."

"Hey," Tony grunted more than said. He was a brick of a soldier with the buzz cut to prove it.

"This is Moscow," Isaac told Tony.

"Oh . . ." Tony's mug shot expression morphed into a wide smile. "I heard about you."

Moscow? Isaac must have been telling stories about my brainless exploits. "Good or bad?"

"In Special Forces, guys get nicknames for cities where they dominated," Isaac said. "Sort of an MVP of a mission."

"And I dominated Moscow?" More like the other way around. It had been my fault Anya had been able to hack into the League files.

"It's a joke," Isaac said. "Sort of."

"Schwarz just likes telling how you jumped off that building."

I hadn't jumped. I'd fallen. But I didn't feel the need to clarify. It felt good to have a guy like Tony look at me like I was some sort of force to be reckoned with.

Boss Schwarz showed up and led me to the on deck waiting area. My chat with Isaac and Tony had pumped me up.

I was feeling optimistic. Until I saw Beth throw her opponent in ring six. Ouch. I hoped I wouldn't have to fight her in front of an audience.

Boss reminded me of the scoring and rules. Each match consisted of three rounds. The first round was five minutes, and the second two rounds lasted two minutes each. Like Kimbal had said, the judges awarded points based on submission, defense, and combat, but it was more complicated than that. Points accumulated for clinch holds, mounts, strikes, blocks, throws, takedowns, and submissions. The most points at the end of all three rounds won the match. In the event of a tie, the judges took into consideration aggressiveness and weight. Penalty points were docked for all kinds of nastiness including eye gouging, illegal strikes, cursing, groin strikes, head butts, hair pulling, and disobeying the ref.

My first match was against a guy named Jones. Isaac called our last names and we walked out to the center of the mat. Isaac checked our gear to make sure we were legal and safe.

"Shake," Isaac said.

We shook.

Isaac positioned us so that we were facing each other about two yards apart. "Okay, boys," Isaac said. "No wedgies, biting, noogies, hair-pulling, slapping, or wet willies. I want a clean and fair fight. You ready?" He looked at each of us.

I nodded. So did Jones.

Isaac pointed to the judges table, nodded, then clapped his hands. "Go."

Jones was shorter than me, and scrappy. He came at me fast, but all his strikes were low three, four, and fives. He liked to kick, but couldn't get his leg high enough to do much damage. I managed to pin him, but he slipped easily out of my ape arms and got off a kick to my back before I could stand.

But I landed plenty of hits, and when the first five minutes ended, I was pleased to see I was ahead eleven to seven.

The next two rounds went by in a flash. We barely had time to do anything before each two-minute round ended. I won the match eighteen to twelve.

Sa-weet!

I won my second match too, but my third opponent, a guy named Kolmorgen, got me on clinch holds. I couldn't get him off me. The guy was like a spider's web. And all those holds added up quickly. I wondered what Beth would do to beat him.

• • •

Much to my own shock—and thrill—I made the finals. Boss said it hadn't been fixed, either. I ranked twenty-three out of fifty. Devin King was ranked twelve. Kolmorgen was nine. Beth four. Some guy named Michaels was ranked first.

Guess who I was up against first thing Saturday morning?

Michaels not Beth. Close one.

Thankfully, today was a double elimination tournament, so I could afford to lose once. Michaels was fighting Devin King in ring three. I took my place on deck and watched more than I stretched.

Michaels was huge—a senior who was nineteen and weighted 205. He had longish blond hair that he wore in a ponytail. How had Beth beaten this beast two years ago? He didn't seem to mind penalty points. He just scored more legal points to make up for them. Tony was refereeing the match, and Michaels was giving him a workout.

Just then Michaels kicked Devin in the head, knocking him out cold. The ref called a penalty. But even with the deduction, Michaels had won. Bess Schwarz helped Devin up, and I was glad to see he was okay. Forget beating this beast. I'd have to stay back and fight smart if I was going to live.

Boss helped Devin over to some guy, then came back to coach me. Tony called my name. Boss patted me on the back, and I walked out to the center of the mat. Tony had me and Michaels shake. With our thick gloves, our fingers barely touched, but it was all the contact I needed. The room grew unnaturally wide, Michaels' head distorting like a pancake, as a glimpse took over my mind's eye: *Michaels and I fought in the far corner of the mat. I had the advantage, then Michaels kicked in my knee. Bone cracked. I howled and dropped to the mat.*

"Hey, Moscow. You ready?" Tony snapped his fingers in front of my face.

I shook to my senses and stepped back. "I forfeit."

Tony's head jerked back. "Really?"

"You afraid?" Michaels asked, his face scrunched up in disgust.

I turned away and walked back to Boss Schwarz. My face was burning, but there was nothing I could do about that.

"What's going on?" Boss asked.

"I forfeited." I grabbed my backpack and started toward the bleachers. A forfeit would bump me into the loser's bracket, but I was okay with that. I wasn't okay with missing the rest of basketball season.

"I can see that, but why?" Boss asked.

"He was going to hurt my knee. Maybe break it."

"Going to? What in blazes you talking about, boy?" Boss Schwarz ran around me so I was forced to face him. "Explain this to—"

Someone pushed me from behind, and I crashed into Boss's chest.

"I'm talking to you, punk!"

I spun around.

Michaels glowered at me, his face flushed. "What's your problem? You scared?"

Boss got between me and Michaels. "Back to your coach, or I'll have you disqualified."

"Yeah, whatever," Michaels said, tossing his head and walking away.

I continued to the bleachers. Everyone was staring. I didn't care. This was one glimpse I was thankful for. The last thing I needed was an injury right before basketball regionals. My team needed me.

I caught sight of Kimbal's orange hair up at the top of the bleachers and waved. He just stared at me, his eyes wide. I'd explain later.

I sat down and waited for the tournament bracket on the wall to be updated. It took a while, and when it finally changed, I choked back a groan.

My next match would be against Beth. Figured.

I looked back to Kimbal, hoping to play it cool, not wanting my uncle to know how much this sucked, but he was gone. Crazy agents, anyway. Maybe he'd spotted the bad guys or something. I hoped so.

REPORT NUMBER: 10

REPORT TITLE: I Take a Tour of the Girl's Locker Room
SUBMITTED BY: Agent-in-Training Spencer Garmond
LOCATION: Los Angeles District LCT Tournament,
Westwood, California
DATE AND TIME: Saturday, December 6, 10:02 a.m.

BETH OF ALL PEOPLE? I MEAN, COME ON. I'd hoped to not
fight her at all. Frankly, I was surprised she'd ended up in the
losers' bracket. Kolmorgen had beaten her—probably with his
clinch holds. Huh. I hadn't lost to Kolmorgen by all that much.

Maybe I *could* beat her.

I looked across the red mat to where Beth sat on the floor.
Mr. S was talking to her, but she was doing her quiet, relaxed
thing, unlike me. I paced back and forth, freaking out. If I lost
here, I was out of the overall. And I hadn't seen anything to
hint that any traitor was coming after me, unless Michaels was
on someone's payroll. I'd have to tell Prière to look into it.

Right now, I needed to calm down. Get through this match
with Beth.

Boss Schwarz fell into the chair on my side of the ring. "You're not going to forfeit again, are you?"

"You're sitting with *me*?" I would have thought Boss would want to coach his former champ.

He waved his hand toward Beth. "She'll be fine. Stopplecamp's going to sit with her."

"Think I'm going to lose?"

"With an attitude like that you already have. Snap out of it." He clapped his hands inches from my face. Guess that's where Beth had learned that. I jumped and stared into Boss's pale blue eyes. "Think strike points, boy, that's all. Numbers. She ain't Beth, she's your foe."

Foe.

I stuck in my mouth piece and walked to the center of the mat where Foe was already waiting. I could do this. Like she'd said, I was stronger than her. I just had to be smarter than her too.

Tony made us shake, then he started the match.

I stepped back cautiously, spreading my feet to get my balance and bending my knees to keep it. Foe did the same. For a long moment we stood motionless, watching each other. The crowd cheered, picking their favorite and calling out my name or Beth's.

I blocked it out, focusing only on my opponent.

Foe.

I came at her with a five-two combo. I liked going left, and it was her weakest defensive point. She blocked it and grabbed my arm. I clinched out of throw danger and leaned forward, hoping to break her balance and take her into mount. We both fell, but Foe popped right back to her feet. I slid onto my side, kicked a five into her gut, grabbed her ankle, and yanked.

She fell, but twisted before she hit the mat and rolled away. I jumped to my feet and crouched into defensive position again.

She sprang at me with a quick one-five-one to the face. I blocked, then sent a five to her stomach, but she darted around my right and I missed. A flash of panic shot through me, knowing my left side was exposed. Thankfully, Foe missed that opportunity and circled around me further.

I twisted back to find her, and she surprised me with a fierce two-blow to my right temple. I staggered back but managed to stay on my feet. Her jaunt around me not only resulted in a throbbing skull, but I lost my balance.

I would not lose it again.

Foe slid forward and fired. Five. Five. Three. One. Two. Five. One-five. One-five.

I blocked everything she had, but stumbled on the last combo. Foe took advantage by sweeping my legs out from under me. I dropped and rolled, but she anticipated my direction and slammed onto my back. I tried to wedge a knee under myself, hoping to roll out of her back-mount hold, but she had both my arms wrenched up my back.

Figs and jam!

My frustration puffed out in a noisy huff. I kept trying, but the time ran out and she still had me. The ref blew the whistle and Beth released me. I jumped up and stormed over to Boss Schwarz. She'd won the match twelve-eight.

Boss threw a towel at my chest. "You didn't stay focused, did you?"

"I did!"

"No. First thing you threw was a five-two combo. You tailored that move for her."

I wiped the soft white cotton over my face. "It's her weakness."

"And *she's* yours. If you're going to win, she's got to be faceless to you."

I sucked down a long swallow of water to avoid having to respond. I threw the towel in a heap at Boss Schwarz's feet. What did he know? She was *not* my weakness.

"You can still win. You were doing fine, but she's quicker than you. Don't get caught too close or she'll trap you. Now, who is she?"

"My foe."

"Atta kid."

Foe. Foe. Foe.

I stepped onto the mat for round two, shook Foe's hand, and rocked back quickly into defensive position.

We faced each other. Foe took a slow step forward. I held steady. In a blur of motion, she jumped at me and sent a five-jab to my temple. I crossed my arms in an X block, spun to the side, and slashed a three at her ribs.

Contact.

"Yes," I breathed aloud to myself.

The hit fueled me, and I came at her with an intricate sequence of moves—the best I had—as fast as I could pitch them out. I whirled from one position to another, but no matter how resourceful my attack, my opponent matched my strikes, blocking everything I sent her way.

Time to up things a bit.

I threw a snap punch/back fist combo, ducked to avoid her five-elbow strike, then snatched her wrist and threw her. She slammed into the mat two yards away and staggered to her feet.

I ran at her and launched a side kick. My foot struck her left hip, and she sagged to her knees. I slid in behind her on one knee and locked her in a bar choke.

My chin rested on her right shoulder, and I breathed hard into her ear. "Tap out, will you?"

"Never." Her body tensed, and she struggled, testing my grip. But my choke was tight. I kept her there until the whistle blew.

I bounced over to my chair, thrilled that I'd won match two five to three. Granted, I was still behind by three and wouldn't see the final scores until it was all over, but at least it felt like I had tied things up.

"Nice work," Boss said. "You're smart to stay off the ground. She can pin anything. Stay on your feet and you have a chance. Try and get some more clinch holds. Those can be easy points."

Tell me about it.

The crowd cheered as Beth and I walked onto the mat for the final time. We shook and stepped into position.

Tony yelled, "Go!"

Beth gave me a shy smile, her dimples tucking in. "You think you can beat me, huh?" she asked, circling to the right. "Maybe you can."

I turned to stay flush with her.

"Focus, Garmond!" Boss's voice was nearly lost in the racket of the arena.

Foe. Opponent. Enemy.

She threw a five to my chest, then came close for a two-elbow to my temple. I dodged left and jammed my knee into her stomach. She sagged and growled like an angry cat.

I couldn't help but smile.

She circled back with a four-side kick. I blocked her leg and kicked out her other ankle. She rolled through her breakfall and came back to her feet. I delivered a chop to her temple, but she blocked my follow up hook to her cheek. She plowed an eight-kick a little too close to a foul for my liking. I backed up to take a breath, but she came at me fast with a five-jab to the ribs. I blocked it and lobbed a two-five back.

Enslaved by the clock, we fought. Strike. Defend. Act. React. As my strength drained, Foe managed a five-punch to my ribs. The blow stung, and I sent one back, but she deflected it with ease. I stepped back again, wanting to breathe, refocus, think.

Again she pressed forward, backing me toward the end of the mat. She grinned, then came at me. Two. Five. Five. Two. One. I staggered, dazed, and felt her familiar grip on my forearm.

Uh-oh.

An easy hip throw sent me to the mat. I shook my head and blinked, but didn't move fast enough. She kneeled on my back, but I managed to get my arms under myself before she could grab one. I could easily get free. She dug her knee into my back. I cringed as I worked my leg up to roll her.

"You're doing good . . . Spencer," she whispered in my ear. "I was wrong about you. Maybe we *should* go out."

I pushed up to roll over and blinked. Was she serious?

The next thing I knew, she'd flipped me onto my back and pinned me in a front strangle, seconds before the whistle blew. I couldn't believe it! The match was over. I'd lost. I knew I had.

Beth jumped up and walked away. I lay flat on the mat, staring at one of the big florescent lamps hanging from the high ceiling. Boss Schwarz's outline appeared above me, black and spotted after I'd stared so long at the light.

Boss extended his hand. I reached for it and he hoisted me to my feet.

"You fought well."

I spit my mouth guard into my hand. "She cheated."

Boss narrowed his eyes. "How's that?"

"She said—" But there was nothing in the rules that prohibited talking during the match. I'd let my guard down. I'd listened to what she'd said—been stupid enough to think she was being serious.

I stopped in front of my chair. I wanted to kick it, watch it fly across the floor. Instead I snagged my towel off the floor and walked away.

"Hey," Boss Schwarz grabbed my shoulder. "Why don't you sit? Take five?"

"I'm going to shower."

"Sit."

I fell onto the chair and stared at the floor while Boss checked me out.

"You feel okay?"

"Fine. Just want to shower."

"Okay." Boss slapped my cheek. "Go shower, then."

I fled.

Gardener and Sasquatch followed me into the men's locker room, but thankfully not the shower itself. They were both dressed as security guards, which allowed them to wear gun belts.

The locker room was like a giant capital E. The first leg was a row of stalls and urinals, the second, lockers, and the third, showers that led out to the pool. The spine was solid mirrors and sinks.

Once I'd washed away the humiliation of being tricked and beaten by a girl in front of five hundred people, I dressed in jeans and a T-shirt and headed back toward Gym One where the finals were being held. I was just about to sit beside Mr. S and Gabe in the bleachers when I heard the announcement.

"Kiplan Johnson to registration. Kiplan Johnson to the registration table, please."

Kip? I looked at Gabe, but he was watching the match in ring three. So was Mr. S.

No one really knew Kip's real name was Kiplan besides the teachers and coaches at school. He hated being called Kiplan.

Could this be it? A trap that only I'd fall for?

I unzipped my backpack and looked for my phone. No sign. I searched the bag two more times and couldn't find my necklace either, though my wallet was there, filled with cash. Not a regular thief, then. I sighed. The only times that my backpack had been out of my sight was when I was in the rings or when I'd been in the shower.

He, she, they—whoever it was, the bad guys—were closing in.

"Lost something?" Mr. S asked.

Yes. My Precious was gone. Again. "Maybe." I zipped my pack. "Be right back." I walked out to the lobby. I kept my distance from the registration table, though, scanning the area for anyone familiar. The only person I recognized was Gardener, just stepping out of the door to Gym One, following me as usual. His slight limp made me think of the mysterious email I'd gotten about his knee replacement surgery, which made me think of my glimpse of Michaels taking me out. I could have been just like Gardner, limping around for the rest of my life.

I caught sight of Devin King, standing in front of the vending machines by the locker rooms. I walked up to him just as he pushed in a dollar bill.

"How's the head?" I asked.

He blew out a noisy breath of air. "I hate that guy." He made his selection and pulled out a Lemon-Lime Gatorade. "How you holding up? Saw that last match against Beth. I don't know what she said to you, but it sure seemed to mess you over."

"Yeah . . . She's a piece of work. "Want to make ten bucks?"

"If you want me to pull a prank on Watkins, you're going to have to pay more than ten bucks. I don't want to be on her bad side."

"This has nothing to do with Beth. The registration desk paged my friend who's not here. Go over there and say you're him. See why they're paging him."

"Why?"

"My reasons are my own." I dug out my wallet from my bag and pulled out two fives.

"Twenty bucks and you got a deal."

"Fine." I traded the fives for a twenty, but I didn't give it to him. "First you do the job."

"Okay." Devin tucked his lanyard into the neckline of his shirt and walked over to the registration table. I looked around me again. No one but Gardener.

Devin made quick work of it and came back to me with a white envelope. "This better not get me in trouble."

"Don't worry about it." I handed him the twenty and snatched the envelope. I ripped it open and pulled out a three by five card.

"Beware the gardener? Free for life servant?" Devin read over my shoulder.

I wanted to turn around and look at the gardener then, but I stayed put. Sure, he could be the traitor. But so could Freeforlifeservant. Why trust him just because he said he was a friend?

Without my phone and my necklace, I couldn't afford to leave the building. I needed to stay where there were people. But I also needed this to end. I needed the traitor to make his move so the good guys could catch him and I could play basketball regionals in peace.

I opened my wallet and pulled out the two fives. "Do me one more favor?" I held out the money. "Go find Boss Schwarz and tell him I'm in the men's locker room, and I'm in trouble." If I could trust anyone, it was Boss.

Devin narrowed his eyes. "Why you in trouble?"

"I'm not now, but I might be. This is important, man. I'm not messing around. Boss knows about it. He'll know what to do."

"Okay. Keep your money, though. I got this." Devin walked toward the gym.

I went the other way. I took my time, not wanting the cavalry to be far behind in case my secret *friend* was right about the gardener.

Like before, Gardener followed me into the locker room. But it wasn't empty. There were at least five guys, plus the door to the laundry was open and an employee was dumping all the used towels into a hamper on wheels.

I doubted Gardener would grab me with this many witnesses present. Figs and jam. What now?

I was going to have to provoke him and see what he did. I turned and sized him up. He looked about five ten and weighed close to two-twenty. Had a bit of a gut. But he was wearing a holster holding two guns that I could see and who knew what else. This might backfire in a big way. Even if he was guilty he could still deny everything.

He could also kill me.

Either way, I had to try and force him to admit his real role as bad guy. If it didn't work, I'd lose nothing. If it did . . .

I dropped my bag and walked straight toward him. His eyes ballooned; he glanced behind him, then back at me.

"So you're Ronald Ashton, right?" I hoped I'd remembered the name right.

His face paled. "Kimbal tell you that?"

"He told me you're the leak."

His Adam's apple bobbed. "That's a lie!"

"They're coming for you now. I was supposed to lure you in here."

Gardener stepped close and pulled one of his guns. "To the pool," he whispered. "Let's go."

Oh . . . kay. I did not expect that to work so well. It was on now. But my backup hadn't arrived yet. I had to think of some way to stall because I certainly didn't want to go toward the pool. I couldn't swim.

I turned as if I was going to comply, then darted through the door to the laundry. It was hot in there and smelled like dryer sheets. I ran without knowing where I was going, hoping I could somehow get back to the men's locker room where Kimbal would come looking.

I passed by the pool office, then turned right down a hallway that came out in the pool bleachers. A half-wall divided the spectator area from the pool. Figs and Jam. Should have gone the other way. Couldn't be helped now.

I banged through the little half-door and jogged out onto the pool apron, taking careful steps. My shoes squeaked on the tile. The pool was empty. I marked a life ring hanging on the wall and wondered if Gardener would throw it to me if I fell in.

"Stop!" Gardener yelled.

I looked back. He was standing at the little half door, gun pointed at me.

"You're not going to shoot me," I said. "You need me alive."

"Which is why I pulled my tranq gun."

Tranq gun and swimming pool. Bad combination.

Ashton jerked the gun to the side and pushed through the half door. "Move it. That way. Toward the exit."

I started that way, but my eyes scanned the place for any other way out. Girl's locker room. Oh yes.

I ran for it, thrilled to put space between me and the water. The gun cracked. I flinched. The tile wall on the other side of the pool splintered. I kept running. Into the tile hallway, over the wet rubber drip mats, past the showers—empty—and into the locker room itself. Also empty.

Come on! I was living every teenage guy's dream right now, and the place was empty.

So unfair.

A quick glance showed the place was set up like the guys' locker rooms, only the E was reversed. I needed to lure Ashton back to the men's locker room. I ran toward the door and darted down the row of stalls. No urinals. I slipped into the middle stall and stood on the toilet.

Gardener wasn't far behind. His footsteps slapped into the locker room and stopped. They started again, coming closer. The locker room door opened, squeaking so loudly it muffled the sound of Gardener's hurried steps.

I looked at the floor, watching for shadows, and spotted my wet footprints on the pink tile. Figs and—

My stall door knocked open, so I jumped on the guy. He turned, slipped into my stall, and my body fell past him. I tried to grab hold and bring him to the floor with me, but . . . well . . . clearly clinch holds were something I needed to work on. I tumbled into the stall hall alone.

"Spencer?"

I turned to look out into the open, mirrored area, and there stood Beth, duffle bag in one hand, towel in the other.

"Why are you in the girl's locker room?" she asked.

"Get rid of her, or she's dead," Gardener whispered. He holstered his tranq gun and drew his pistol.

Oh, well. This was working out nicely.

"I wanted to talk to you," I said. Because making myself look like a perverted stalker was the best I could come up with on the spot, okay?

I pushed to my feet and made sure that I got a full step closer to the main room in the process. "What you did in that last round . . ."

Beth dropped her bag. "I told you a hundred times, Tiger, this isn't a regular sport. LCT isn't fair because life isn't fair."

"It was a low blow." And I meant it. But I turned my body enough so that my right arm would be hidden from Ashton and inched forward a bit more.

"Get over it. You could've beaten me, Spencer. You were awesome out there. But, as usual, you lost your focus."

I thumbed behind me, but it probably looked like I was pointing at myself. "Well . . . competition has turned you into a machine."

She snorted. "Like *you* can talk. Have you seen yourself play basketball?"

I inched toward her again. "That's totally diff—"

"Enough!" Ashton stepped out of the stall and pressed the gun to the back of my head. My shoulders went up instinctively, as did my hands. "We're leaving. Girl, you come over here."

"Okay," Beth said, her eyes wide, her bottom lip trembling.

Nice. Mr. Ashton-Gardener was about to meet his match. He fisted the back of my shirt and pulled me behind him, keeping the gun against the back of my skull. He motioned Beth toward us. "Quickly, or I'll shoot him."

Beth moved. I suppose I could have tried to knock away the gun, or steal his other one, but stories that Kip's dad had told me of guns going off and people dying had me a little gun shy.

Ashton ushered Beth into stall. "On your knees, facing the toilet." He stepped back and waved the gun at me. "Tie her up."

"With what?"

He stepped back and started fumbling with his belt buckle.

"Really?" I said. "I thought you were a cop. This is the best you can do?"

His face purpled. "It wasn't supposed to happen here! We had plans. Plans you ruined." He yanked his belt out in one long pull and tossed it to me. "Bind her hands and feet together."

I looked at Beth, who was mouthing something to me. "Are you kidding me? She's not a contortionist."

"Make it happen," Ashton said.

Beth was still trying to tell me something, so I said, "It's a tiny stall."

"Kid . . ." He scowled and breathed a few short breaths through his nose. Then he pulled the tranq gun and shot Beth in the back. The impact knocked her into the crack between the bowl and the stall's wall. She stirred for a minute, then collapsed on the floor of the stall.

I yelled, totally taken off guard. "What'd you do that for?"

"Eliminating complications. Now, let's go."

He backed out of the stall hall and motioned me past him, deeper into the locker room, back toward the showers and pool entrance. I went. The other agents couldn't be far now. And with Beth as a witness—if she was okay—they could arrest Ashton and hopefully find out who "we" was.

It was time to lose the shadow.

I walked past the lockers and turned down the bank of showers. I let my sneaker snag on the rubber drip mat and tripped, falling on my knees under the first showerhead. I cranked the knob, and the water came on, shooting over my head and drenching Ashton. He gasped. I stepped to the side of the flow, pushed off the wall, and side-kicked his right knee.

I'd never heard such a horrible scream.

He went down, dropped his gun, clutched his knee.

I kicked the gun away and reached for the tranq gun, but he got to it first. So I sat on him, trapping him in the mount position. I applied a left handed choke to get his gun arm. Then I moved off to his right side, pulled his arm with me, rolled my left leg over his face, and laid back, getting him in an armbar. This put me on my back with my legs extended sideways over him, and I had his arm trapped between my legs with the gun at my face, pointing straight above my head. I pulled a little, forcing his arm back until he cried out and dropped the gun. It clunked to the rubber mats just over my left shoulder.

I could break his arm. I probably should. I doubted I could hold him until someone came in and could go for help. He might be hurt, but he was well trained, rusty or not.

I did my best to hold the armbar with my left hand as I reached my right hand over my body toward the gun. I managed to grab it, but Ashton got leverage against my one-handed armbar and hitchhiked, turning up on his shoulder and pushing his back against the back of my legs. He scooted along the floor on his side, unwinding himself from my grip, and suddenly got me in a side control position.

But I had the gun.

I reached over his head and fired at his back. The gun clicked.

Ashton laughed, his head down by my left armpit. "Only had two darts, kid."

I threw the gun and pulled a third one from the back of his belt. It was black and yellow and tiny. A Taser. It had a safety switch on the side. So, I flicked it and fired. There was no recoil. It sounded like a balloon popped, and then like a rattlesnake. Ashton grunted and released me. I unthreaded myself and left him there, ran back out through the pool and into the men's locker room. I met Sasquatch in the hall to the showers.

He pointed his gun at me, then quickly lowered it. "He's here, Kimbal."

"It's Ashton," I said over my own panting. "I Tased him. He's in the girl's locker room. You can get there through the pool."

"Bridges, Stern, with me." Sasquatch ran out the way I'd come in. Two guys followed.

Kimbal approached me. "When Schwarz told me you were in the locker room, I assumed that meant the *men's* locker room."

"It did." I took a deep breath, then remembered Beth. "He shot Beth with a tranq gun. She's in a stall in the girl's locker room."

Kimbal turned from me and touched his ear. "We need a medical team in the girl's locker room right now." He straightened and rubbed his finger and thumb over his eyes. "Did it knock her out?"

"Yeah, but . . . It's just a tranquillizer," I said. "She'll be fine, right?"

"Tranqs are iffy. It's not like in the movies, Garmond. It's all about the dose. Too small, your man doesn't go down. Too high, you could kill him. My guess is Ashton knew your weight and tailored that dose for you. And you've got at least thirty pounds on Watkins. I'm also betting this was the same stuff they shot you with before."

Kimbal's words hit me like a taser, electric and gripping. Beth could be dead.

Because of me.

REPORT NUMBER: 11

REPORT TITLE: I Get Lectured by a French Guy
SUBMITTED BY: Agent-in-Training Spencer Garmond
LOCATION: UCLA Medical Center, 757 Westwood Plaza, Los Angeles, California
DATE AND TIME: Saturday, December 6, 3:56 p.m.

BETH WAS TAKEN TO THE RONALD REAGAN UCLA Medical Center in Westwood. I followed in a sedan with Kimbal, praying—yes, praying—that she was okay.

After an hour of sitting in the waiting room, Prière showed up. He pulled me to a private corner to get the full story.

After I'd given him the scoop he said, "I must confess, Spence, I am very disturbed."

Uh oh. "You are? Why?"

"It is true, in this mission we were hoping that the traitor would come forward. We had reason to believe that he would. But we did not ask you to risk your life to draw him out."

Oh. "I just . . . wanted it to end. It *needed* to end. Now it has." Sort of. "But *you* chose to use me as bait. And you're the one who put an ultimatum on this day. It had to be my final stand. Plus, why would he kill me? You said it yourself. They want information, the prophecy or whatever."

"This Freeforlifeservant who sends you messages. You must begin reporting these. He might not be the friend you think him to be. And I am still unconvinced that you are safe living in this place."

"Yeah, well, I don't mean to be rude, Prière, but I don't care." The man's eyes widened, so I kept talking. "I mean, Christians are supposed to have faith, to trust God with their life, right? Don't you trust God?"

"Oui. Of course I trust him."

"Then let this play out. Let them come for me. I'm not afraid." I was a little afraid, actually, but he didn't have to know that.

"Beth Watkins?" a deep voice said.

I looked up. A doctor was standing at the front of the waiting room. I jumped up and ran over to him, beating Kimbal by three good paces. Please let her be okay.

"She's awake," the doctor said, and relief swelled through me. "The sedative was iVitrax. It's a popular street drug that induces hallucinations, but in large doses can knock out a person pretty fast."

Yeah . . . I'd heard that.

"She overdosed, actually," the doctor said, "so we need to monitor her for a few days. Have her parents arrived?"

"Her father, not yet," Kimbal said.

"Once he arrives we can see about letting in some visitors," the doctor said.

I tried to go sit with Kimbal after that, but Prière called me back over. "Very well, Spence. We will give this a little more time. See if our people can get Ashton to reveal anything of use. I am pleased that you are so very brave, but I must raise one point that I think you have neglected to consider."

"What's that?"

"You might not be afraid of being captured. And that is fine. But once you are captured, and perhaps tortured—maybe you give up the information these people desire, and maybe you don't. But when all of that has come to an end, then you should be afraid. Because once they have determined that they have no further use for you, they will kill you. I do not want that to happen. Remember, Spence. God will do what he will do. Maybe he will save you. Or maybe he will allow the consequences of your recklessness to end your life. I cannot say. But I do not gamble with life. And you should not do so either."

Point taken. I should really stop trying to outthink Christians where God was concerned. Clearly I didn't fully understand how the big guy did things. A little more prayer might help, I supposed.

Prière was letting me stay, for now. I might stink at LCT, and I wasn't any good at getting the girl, but I wasn't helpless. I'd drawn out Ashton. I'd proven that I could do this spy thing. And now, I'd search Grandma's room for clues about my mom. I'd find out what really happened to her. And the baddies? They could just bring it, because I'd be ready. I'd proven to Prière and Kimbal and Mr. S that I could take care of myself.

THE END

Spencer will return in *Project Gemini*

ACKNOWLEDGEMENTS

Much gratitude to the following individuals: Jeff Gerke for letting me do this project. Amanda Luedeke for supporting me and my crazy ideas. Kirk DouPonce for designing an amazing book cover. Jeremy Gwinn and Lucinda Tilstra for modeling. Rebecca Luella Miller for being my editor. Chris Kolmorgen for that last-minute brainstorming session. Kerry Nietz for creating the ebooks and coaching me in ISBN and ebook uploading. Angie Lusco for being my medical source. Emely DeLeon for her help with Spanish. Melanie Dickerson, Stephanie Morrill, Shellie Neumier, and Nicole O'Dell for moral support. Brad Williamson for being amazing and putting up with my crazy questions and crises. And to Kevin and Wendy Haydon for adopting *two* children who needed a home.

 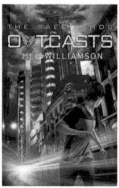 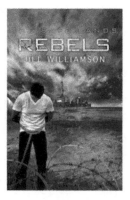